ALL SHE EVER DESIRED

A CEDAR VALLEY NOVEL

CHRISTINA BUTRUM

Pat -
Enjoy Conner + Megan!
♡ Christina
Butrum

Edited by: Lawrence Editing

Cover by: Amanda Walker PA and Designs

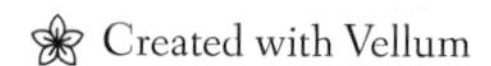
Created with Vellum

For my readers who fell in love with Cedar Valley.

1

At the time, coming back to Cedar Valley had sounded like a good idea. Now, not so much. Over the last few months, he had managed to screw up every chance at making things better between him and his father. The conflict dated back before his venture to bigger and better things in Colorado.

Who knew his father would hold a grudge against him this long for leaving this small town—he sure hadn't. Not that knowing what he knew now would have changed a damn thing, but the thought of an actual stable relationship with his father sounded nice.

"What can I get you to drink?"

The woman's voice pulled him from his distracting thoughts. He had managed to make his way to Levy's right after his shift ended at the department. Working doubles to help Adam cover shifts, he was worn out. The work, along with the family conflict, was wearing on him.

"The usual," he said, tipping up the brim of his ball cap as he locked his eyes with the strawberry blonde's. So much had changed between them and he found himself to blame for that, too.

After shrugging, she said, "You've been gone so long I've forgotten what your usual is."

"It hasn't been *that* long," he spat out, not even checking the defensiveness in his tone. She was probably right, though. He'd been gone for two years, and no matter how one looked at it, it had been a long time away from the small town life. The glare she gave him told him she begged to differ. "Meg, you act like I've been gone for years."

Pushing off the counter, she turned to grab a glass from the stack, leaning next to the tap. "Because it felt that way."

Although her voice was just above a mumble, he heard her loud and clear. "Hey, look, I didn't mean to make our friendship suffer," he said, reaching for his drink while keeping his eyes fixed on hers. She used to be good at hiding emotion, but now he could see it plain as day written all over her face and shading her eyes with hurt and anger. "I was only trying to better my life."

"Typical you," she said, shaking her head with no sign of sugar-coating her brutal honesty. He admired her for that. She was a strong female who knew exactly what she wanted in life—something he had never thought twice about. All he knew involved fires, chasing fires, and more fires. Her five-year plan was stable and clear, whereas his was on shaky grounds with no guarantee. "Always thinking of yourself."

"What's that supposed to mean?" he asked, defensive only because this wasn't her usual attitude toward him. Something else was going on and he was determined to figure it out. "I'm still the same ol' Conner."

He offered her his sly wink with his hellacious grin—the grin that dropped panties and had women begging to come home with him at night. One-night stands were a thing of the past. In Colorado, it was easy to find the girls who were okay with the terms of no-strings-attached. Here in this small town, finding someone to tangle the sheets with was more difficult than he wished. Plus, he refused to allow his sexual appetite to dampen his reputation as a dependable firefighter.

"Look, I want to know why you're so angry with me," he said, trying to grab her attention back from her phone. It was easy to see she was trying her hardest to not have this conversation with him. But something was wrong and he cared, regardless of what she thought. "Hey," he said, standing in order to reach across the counter in an attempt to pull her near him. "What's going on?"

Her eyes glanced up from the bright screen she had been focused on for the last few minutes. "Who says I'm angry?"

Pulling the barstool up before sitting back down, he said, "Well, the tone of your voice says a lot."

"Look, I'm just trying to do my job and go home, okay?" she said, playing on his words he'd used all night. "I don't have time to have a heart-to-heart discussion about you and your so-called entitlement."

"Entitlement?" He shook his head and leaned forward on his elbows. "Meg, what are you even talking about?"

Shaking her head, she turned and began scrubbing down the countertop a few feet down from him. "You just don't get it."

"No, I guess I don't," he said, tipping back the last of his drink before he silently asked for a refill by raising his empty glass. "Why don't you explain *it* to me since I don't get *it*?"

They'd gone back years. Years long ago when they were

still in diapers blabbering nonsense back and forth. They'd become the best of friends, but he couldn't remember having an argument without knowing what the hell it was about. Hell, she was like one of the guys. Emotions never got in the way of their friendship. Until now.

"What do you wanna know? The part where you left me hanging behind, or the part where you constantly run from your problems?" She was pissed, and though he had no idea what triggered this conversation, he knew she had every right to be upset because he lost connection with her while he was out in Colorado chasing bigger and better...no, not better, but definitely bigger things. But running from his problems? Was that what she truly thought he had done? If so, she was wrong. That was not what he had done at all.

"I'm sorry." He had nothing else to say. He wanted to defend his reason for leaving, but he knew this had nothing to do with himself and everything to do with her feelings getting hurt by his selfish move out west.

"No," she said, shaking her head. "You're not sorry. If you were sorry, you would have stayed in touch with this town, with me, regardless of your unstable relationship with your dad. Regardless of chasing bigger fires."

"Don't bring my relationship with my father into this." Anger struck a nerve far deeper than her words. The relationship between him and his father was unhinged and the gap between them would never get filled at the rate they were going, but that was between them and no one else. This argument here and now was about her. Him. Whoever and whatever. But not about his father.

She shrugged. He hated when people shrugged instead of responding after he'd say something. What the hell had gotten into her? She was perfectly fine earlier on shift at the station. Nothing drastic had happened during their shift.

"I'm just saying."

"Saying what? That you're upset I left you behind and lost touch with you while I was there and not here?"

Her eyes were filled with hurt, possibly anger, but mostly hurt as she glanced up at him once again from her phone.

"Will you put down the damn phone and have a damn conversation with me?" His tone was sharp, his anger getting the best of him as he motioned for her to follow through with what he'd asked her to do. "You have every right to be pissed at me, but dammit, I had no choice."

"Oh, you had a choice," she said, her words bitter. "You had options and you refused to look past that tunneled vision of yours."

He was taken aback by her choice of words. Where the hell was this coming from? He wanted to make things right, but right now he needed to finish his drink and head out before words were spoken that couldn't be taken back.

"I have no clue what you're talking about, but I gotta get going," he said, slapping a twenty on the counter. "Keep the change."

Only when she said nothing more, he turned and walked toward the door. There was no telling where this conversation had taken them tonight, but he was sure of one thing—she was stubborn and refused to let anyone else call the shots around here.

The drive back to Adam's place, a place he temporarily called home, was quiet as he turned the events from tonight over and over in his mind. He still had no idea what had gotten into her. What had made her act like he was a selfish person. He was far from that, wasn't he? He worked as a firefighter, for Pete's sake. A career that expected every ounce of selfless actions and sacrifices.

Pulling into the driveway, he turned off the headlights and killed the engine. Most likely everyone was probably fast asleep because it was well after ten and the kids had school tomorrow.

Climbing the porch steps one at a time, trying not to make too much noise, he sat down on the swing. He wasn't tired and going into a dark, quiet house didn't sound appealing at the moment. Reaching into the tight pocket of his Wranglers, he pulled out his cell phone.

Wanting to text her, he tapped on her name, causing her face to fill his screen as his phone dialed her number. Quickly tapping the screen to end the call, the phone fumbled out of his hand and the last thing he heard before it fell apart at his feet was the sound of Megan's sweet voice.

Damn. He'd had too much to drink tonight. He should've never gone to Levy's after his shift. Instead, he should've come home and helped Tyler practice his tackles like he had promised the young boy. Once again, he had let someone down and he was sure he would hear about it tomorrow.

Putting his phone back together, he decided to call it a night and shoved it back into his pocket. Nothing good would come out of texting her anyway. Hell, the argument they'd had at Levy's had been nothing like they'd ever had before. Sure, they'd had plenty of spats growing up, but nothing that couldn't be settled over ice cream or beer. Now, he wasn't sure what would make this better. He had said sorry. Apologizing wasn't his strong suit. He apologized when he was in the wrong, but even then, it was difficult to admit he was wrong.

But with Megan it was different. His words had escaped his mouth without effort. Talking to her had always been so easy. He didn't know what he'd do if he couldn't make things right between them. Losing her would be equivalent to losing family. He cherished what they shared in this friendship and he wouldn't let it end without a fight.

Deciding once again to call it a night, he stood and walked to the screen door. The vibration of his phone startled him, causing him to let go of the door. Hearing it crack against the frame, he cringed as he reached into his pocket for his phone.

Her face, once again, filled the screen and he couldn't help but see something more than a friend staring back at him.

Against his better judgement, he swiped his thumb across the screen and answered the phone. Whatever this phone call would accomplish would have to be something more than doing nothing at all.

2

The call she received from Conner should have been ignored. Butt dials happen all the time. The possibility of his phone dialing her number while in his tight front pocket of his jeans was incredibly slim to none, but she wouldn't believe for a second he had every intention of calling her.

The conversation, more like an argument, they had tonight during her shift at Levy's was a bit heated and she couldn't help feeling like she had come off as a complete bitch. Something she was used to, but not with Conner. He was different. He wasn't like all the others who pissed her off. He meant something more than that to her.

He just didn't understand the seriousness of their friendship and had proved it tonight when he said a quick apology. Maybe she had no right to be upset with him. Maybe she was making this a lot bigger than what it was.

Looking at her phone, his goofy grin filled her screen. A picture she had taken right before he had left for Colorado. The night he had promised they would stay in touch. The night he had told her there was more out there for him to discover and he was ready to branch out and become the best firefighter he possibly could be.

Swiping a tear off her cheek, she chased those memories away.

Answering the call, she said, "Hello."

"Shit."

Call ended. Staring at her phone, trying to process what just happened and why he would call just to hang up on her, she fought against the urge to call him back. If it was important, he would call back—or not—it wasn't in her control. This whole thing between them, whatever it was, wasn't about control or changing his way of doing things. Conner would be Conner no matter how many people disagreed with him.

She wanted nothing more than to make him realize what he had in Cedar Valley. Everything. He could have it all and more if he put his mind to it. If he faced his conflicts head-on instead of running from them, or towering over them with the authority of avoidance, he could have what he'd been spending his whole life chasing after. Right here in Cedar Valley.

Growing up in Cedar Valley, she knew the small town limited its offerings. But joining the department, actively volunteering on the service, the town offered a lot more than what was visible to the eye on first glance. She had learned the true meaning of respect and responsibility—something many her age disregarded. In a short time, she had worked her ass off to prove that a female was capable of pulling off anything a man could do. It took dedication and an abundance of determination and strength, but she knew nothing more gratifying than to prove her worth to the town she loved.

Staring at her phone, she decided on calling him back.

Their friendship was worth more than a sudden hang up, right? Dialing his number, she allowed it to ring a few times, and right before she imagined him answering, she clicked it off. She didn't know what to say to him. Their argument had been ridiculous, and she was most likely overreacting, but for right now, she needed to sleep on it. She would talk to him in the morning, or whenever she saw him again—only if he was willing to talk to her.

Shrugging off the thoughts racing through her mind, she pulled back the covers and climbed into bed. Tomorrow would start early, and the way it looked, it would be a long, drawn out day with tension and hard work.

She had every intention of making Conner realize what he had missed out on while in Colorado. Where he fought big fires and faced a broader selection of challenges, she felt it had been too much for him. Not that he was weak, but a person could only handle so much trauma before it buried its claws in deep and left scars unhealed and bared for all to see. On the outside, he appeared okay, but she could see through him and she knew the conflicts were running deep, clawing their way to the surface. It was only a matter of time before they were exposed and it wouldn't be pretty. She wasn't sure of what would happen, or how, or even when, but the one thing she did know, he would need someone there for him and that someone would be her.

3

Conner tugged the hoses from the trucks, lining them up in front of the abandoned house, condemned and ready for them to burn. Today was training day and he was determined to test the best compared to others on the department. He'd spent time in Colorado, learning the ins and outs of running full shifts with back to back fires and knowing the basics to survive not only the first shift, but all of them—some shifts dragged on longer than expected. It was a game of survival and he had taken it seriously. Chasing fires ran in his blood. Dating back to his great-grandfather, skipping his grandfather, and landing on his father and Adam, and then him, firefighting was the life the Jacobsen boys grew up knowing. They had big shoes to fill at a young age and they had everything to prove.

"Hey," he called out to one of the newbies. "Grab that line there and get it ready."

"What line?" the newbie hollered back, a confused look creasing his brow line. Conner had to give it to him, though. This kid was just that—a kid. Just barely turned sixteen and wanted to volunteer for the summer. In Conner's opinion, it was better for young kids to volunteer rather than raise hell in town, winding up in trouble and tallying up community service hours. Volunteering did them good. Kept them honest and on a straight and narrow path.

Conner jogged over to the kid, who was now standing between the two trucks, still trying to figure out what line Conner was talking about. "This one," Conner said, reaching out for the hose and giving it a quick jerk to unlatch it. "Adam will be starting the fire in a few minutes. We have to make sure everything is set up and ready to go. Welcome to your first day of actual training, kid."

The young kid nodded, still looking lost in his own thoughts.

"Look, you're going to want to relax and pay careful attention," Conner explained. Pointing to the condemned house, he said, "This house fire's going to be staged, but we'll play it off as the real deal. You either sink or swim. You fight the fire or you die."

The kid's eyes widened in fear.

Conner patted him on the back. "Hey, no worries, you'll do just fine."

Conner chuckled as he ran the last line out and made sure the hoses were hooked up and ready to go as soon as Adam gave the command. Taking a last-minute scan of his surroundings, he didn't see Megan. If he was honest, he had expected her to be the first on scene, staged and ready to go. She was a badass medic, crossover firefighter. In all honesty, she could kick his ass in simulations and test times, but he kept those thoughts to himself—quiet and sealed away. He wouldn't allow anyone to know he had doubts when it came to a girl beating him at anything.

Making a quick check on the newbie, he asked the kid if he was ready.

With a nod, the kid said, "I was born ready."

Conner couldn't help but chuckle at the kid's sudden change in confidence. This kid would make a helluva firefighter if he stuck with it. Conner had advised him it took dedication and more determination than an average person could muster sometimes, but at the end of the day, there wasn't a damn thing more rewarding than giving back to the community.

He watched Adam hustle toward them. It was only a matter of time before the fire would start. A small detonation inside would excite them and it would be game on. The equivalent of gunfire at a race.

"Where's Megan?" Conner asked, still wondering why she wasn't there.

"I'm right here," she said, walking up behind the crowd, a smile on her face. "You didn't think I'd miss a chance to kick your ass at putting out this fire, did you?"

Conner shook his head. The confidence she exuded was something else. Tossing a wink with a shit-eating grin her way, he said, "We'll see who's kicking whose ass."

She tossed her head back laughing, making it known she was calling his bluff. Sometimes, he had to let her win, but now? Nope, not a chance. She was going down.

"Everyone ready to take care of this place?" Adam asked, pointing back to the rickety old house with hanging boards and missing shutters and shingles.

"10-4, Chief," they all said in unison.

Adam nodded and within a minute, a spark set fire to the rundown house. Standing back watching, they waited for the flames to engulf the structure, ready more than ever to take back full control of the flickering flames.

Conner watched Megan toss the hose over her shoulder and take off in a dead sprint toward the flames. No way he'd let her get a head start over him. Reaching down, he grabbed his own line and took off in a full-on chase after her while hollering back to the newbie to grab a hose and do something.

It didn't take long for the fire to show its roaring aggressiveness through the structure of the old farm house. Sectioned off in a row, the squad had the flames cornered and within minutes, the flames were controlled.

He caught Megan taking subtle glances his way. He shook his head and laughed. That girl was all about competition and kicking ass. There was no way he could ever win against her. She'd have him beat twice over before he could even say "go." He'd call a truce later, but right now, he'd enjoy watching her fight these flames alongside him.

Vibration rattled his suit. Beeping blasted from pagers surrounding him. "Cedar Valley Fire Department and Medics, you're needed on highway one twenty-two at intersection two-twentieth for an MVC. I repeat, you're needed at the intersection of two-twentieth and one twenty-two for a single car collision involving a deer. No major injuries reported at this time, but deputies are requesting assistance."

Adam glanced back at Conner, who in turn looked at Newbie and Megan. Rounding them up, Adam hollered for the senior guys to stay back while the four of them responded to the car accident.

Yanking off his helmet, he jogged to the truck. The look on the newbie's face was of sheer terror and uncertainty. "Don't worry, you're good. Just follow command and do what you're asked. You'll be just fine."

Newbie nodded, climbing in the back of the truck before securing himself in place. Conner held the door open for Megan as she hustled into an empty seat next to

Newbie. Conner told her to be nice to the kid as he offered her a wink before shutting the door and climbing in front with Adam.

"How bad do you think it is?"

Adam shrugged. "Hard to say. It depends."

"On?"

"The size of the buck. The speed of the vehicle upon impact," Adam said, pulling the truck away from the abandoned house and steering it in the direction of highway one twenty-two.

"That's one thing I didn't have a lot of in Colorado," Conner said.

"Car accidents?" Adam asked, offering him a raised brow.

"Car accidents, yes. Deer, not so much," Conner said, taking a look in front of them as they rolled up on scene. "Most of the accidents out there were from boulders and speeding. Not paying attention."

Adam chuckled and shook his head. "Yeah, I guess it'd be hard to dodge a boulder on the highway."

"A lot of people got lucky. Plenty of falling rocks, but none landed on the roof of the car, thankfully. That would've made for a nasty call."

"Ready?" Adam looked back at Newbie and Megan. Conner glanced back, the newbie looking whiter than a ghost. He nodded reassurance toward him, but the kid was running on adrenaline. "There's nothing better than your first call, kid. Just follow commands and you'll be fine."

Conner looked back at Newbie. "Told ya so. Hang with me and you'll learn stuff."

Megan looked at the kid and said, "Don't listen to Conner. He has no idea what he's talking about."

The kid laughed and shook his head. Succeeding in

releasing the kid's apprehension of the unknown, Conner smiled. Anytime he could make someone's first call easier, he'd do it.

Hopping out in unison, they gathered their gear and made their way to the car. Deputies on scene advised them the deer was taken care of, dispatched with one shot to put it out of its misery. Conner witnessed Megan's wrinkled nose, agreeing they would've been fine without the details of the aftermath.

"Go ahead and clear the car for the medics, Conner," Adam hollered over the squawk of static and squabble on the radio. "Megan, stand by for gas leaks and any signs of a fire."

Conner did his job, making sure the car was cleared for the medics, whose sirens blared in the distance. He glanced back at Megan, giving her a thumbs-up to let her know the car was good. She nodded and assisted the ambulance when it got on scene. A medic in his early forties made his way to the car and asked if the car was cleared. And only after Conner nodded, he ducked inside and talked to the driver, asking her if anything hurt or if she had hit her head. Bumps and small scratches covered her face, she appeared shaken up, but other than that, she looked okay.

Conner turned to walk back toward Adam and Megan, who were showing the newbie the ins and outs of managing a minor car accident such as this one. Walking back to his squad members, a loud gunshot fired behind him.

"What the..." Conner turned, examining the scene displayed behind him. One medic had dragged the driver out of the car, who was now lying on the ground next to the totaled vehicle, and another charged toward Conner.

"I thought you said this car was clear!" Shouting with anger, raged fists darted in Conner's direction.

Holding his hands up in defense, he told the medic to take it easy. He couldn't believe what had happened. And of course, his brother was on his way over to break up the confrontation.

"What the hell are you letting him clear cars for if he doesn't actually clear the damn things?"

The medic was pissed, Adam was pissed, glaring in Conner's direction. A simple task he had forgotten to do—clip the battery wire to prevent a delayed airbag deployment.

"Go back to the patient, I'll take care of this," Adam said, pointing the medic in the direction of the vehicle.

"Easy for you to say. You didn't 'bout lose your damn head!" the medic huffed as he turned and stomped away, following the direction back to his patient.

Conner glanced at Megan, a sympathetic look on her face. She had to understand it was a simple mistake—one he would never make again. She shook her head. Disappointment lined her face and it made him question whose side she was on.

"What the hell were you thinking?" Adam asked, jabbing a pointed finger into Conner's chest. "You could've caused that medic serious injuries."

"Come on, it didn't, though," Conner said, trying his damnedest to get Adam off his case. "He got the driver out in time and all is fine."

"Fine? You think that's fine?" Adam pointed in the direction of the totaled vehicle now with a deployed airbag. "You had one job. One damn job, Conner!"

The urge to shrug his shoulders, pass this off as just an accident crossed his mind. That was exactly what this was, an accident. It wasn't his fault he had forgotten to clip the battery wires. Damn. Yeah, it would've been bad if the medic had gotten hurt, but he didn't. All was fine and they had a job to finish.

"You act like nothing you do has consequences. Like everything that goes wrong will be taken care of and no sweat off your back," Adam said with his face in Conner's. "Like it wouldn't have been your problem. It would've been my responsibility to clean up, huh?"

"No," Conner said, catching a glance at Megan, who was avoiding the confrontation the best she could as she looked away. He looked Adam in the eye and said, "You need to take it easy. It was a mistake. A simple mistake in a minor accident. It's not that big of a deal."

"Not a big deal?" Adam's face scrunched in anger, twisted with rage, and his fists doubled at his sides.

"Not as big as you're making it," Conner said, shrugging off his brother's confrontation as he turned away.

"Conner, we're not through with this conversation," Adam shouted after him, grabbing their gear and rounding up equipment to head back to the station. "I mean it."

"Okay, Dad."

Conner didn't want issues with his brother. It was bad enough to have their father on his case, let alone another person on him for something that was a simple mistake.

"What'd you say?" Adam was on Conner's backside faster than he realized. Adam spun him and shoved him into the truck. "You cut your shit out or get off my service."

Conner stood silent, facing Adam's rage head-on with no fear. He couldn't care less about Adam's insecurities with being compared to their father. He wasn't here to kiss ass and make their lives easier than they already were. As far as he was concerned, his dad and brother had it easier than he ever did. He couldn't just fit in and make things work. He couldn't just advance to fire chief and be accepted. He had struggled to find acceptance—to fit in—and it had all started when his own father had chased him out of town. Not physically, but with his words and cold shoulder actions.

The drive back to the station was quiet and awkward. Conner knew he crossed the line and there was no way of erasing what had been said and done. The story of his life. Nothing new.

Unloading the truck, tossing his gear to the side, Megan walked up and looked at him. Her eyes said so much more than she was willing to say and that was okay. He didn't care what she thought of him at the moment. She had no idea.

"You can't act like this," she said, tossing her gear on the ground next to the truck. "It'll ruin your career and you'll have nothing."

"Whatever you say," he said, shrugging off her words, not wanting to dismiss her, but not caring what advice she had to give him. Like he had said, she had no idea.

"Conner, my office," Adam hollered out the door, waving him over. "Now."

Without looking back at Megan, he walked toward Adam's office. No rush. He could wait to get his ass chewed.

Closing the door behind him, Conner made his way into Adam's office. The last place he wanted to be was in a small room and cornered. Confrontation wasn't on his list of favorite things either.

"What were you thinking?" Adam asked, sitting in the chair behind his desk, not waiting for Conner to take the chair across from him. "Where's your head at?"

Standing, not wanting to sit, Conner would wait out the conversation. Depending on how it went would make the final decision to sit or not.

Crossing lines and pressing his luck was something Conner was good at. His father had reiterated that through his younger years. A bullhead, determined to make such a difference, not realizing how much of a mess he created in order to make the change—sometimes making things worse. Like now. Nothing had changed.

"What do you want me to say?" Conner asked, not wanting to argue. He was tired of explaining, defending his actions, and thinking things were changing. He'd been wrong numerous times and every time, he somehow expected not to be wrong. "I did what I had to do. I cleared the car."

Adam shook his head, the disappointment evident on his face. Conner couldn't help but compare the facial expressions Adam made with those of his father's. Similar in many ways, he was envious of Adam's relationship with their father.

"What do you think clear the car means?"

"Clear it," Conner said.

"Don't get smart with me," Adam said, his words stern and his brows furrowed. Adam was quick to a temper, something that had changed over the course of the last year. Conner blamed all of the wedding talk. The thought of a wedding sounded overwhelming and stressful as it was. Add in working numerous shifts to cover the fire department and trying to balance two kids in the equation, Conner could see why his brother was stressed. The man was getting married in eight months and it seemed to be right around the corner.

"I'm not trying to be," Conner explained. "I checked for

leaking fluids and other hazards. The battery crossed my mind, but I got distracted and spaced it off."

Adam leaned back in his chair and crossed his arms. "Conner, man, I can't have you getting distracted. It's life or death out there. I can't have you risking lives. Yours. Mine. Or theirs."

He knew death all too well. The fires in Colorado had taught him what to expect the last year of his service. The fire that had quickly spread through the forest, had claimed two of his best friends he'd made there. They were like the brothers he'd never had. Brothers he'd wished he'd had, but God never heard his plea. Sure, he had Adam, but their age difference set them farther apart throughout the years after they left single digits.

"I know what death is. I know the risks of this job," Conner said, knowing his defensive tone would keep the argument going longer.

"I know you do, and I'm sorry about what happened in Colorado, but it's my job here to make sure my squad goes home safe every night, along with everyone on scene. I need you to understand that. I also need you to keep your focus on what's in front of you and not everything that's behind you."

"I'm not distracted with my past," Conner said, again his tone edgy, and Adam picked up on it. Adam leaned forward and rested his elbows on the desk. "I'm serious. I don't need you telling me how to do my job or how to live my life."

Adam adjusted in his seat, pulling his chair closer to the desk before saying, "I'm not trying to tell you how to live your life. Trust me, it wouldn't work anyway. You've got your own brain. I'm just asking you to use it and think about the aftermath of your actions. That's all."

"Are we done?" This had turned into a waste of time. Conner had other places to be, like out there talking to Megan for one. They'd crossed paths last night at the bar and wires had gotten crossed. He wanted her to know he wasn't the asshole she thought he had turned into. Sure, he had his moments, but deep down he cared. Sometimes, he cared too much. A weakness that led him to troubled territory more than once. A weakness that would lead him to risking everything to prove he knew what the hell he was doing, and the last thing he needed was for someone to tell him otherwise.

"Sure," Adam said, standing to lead him out of the office. Patting him on the shoulder, Adam opened the door and led him out into the hallway. "Just do me a favor and pay attention. Make wise decisions and don't be so impulsive."

The conversation had ended for Conner when he had asked if it was done. He turned the corner and made his way back to the garage. He needed to find Megan and try to make amends to fix their friendship before things got more out of control than they already were.

4

Watching Conner walk into Adam's office tempted her to follow him in. She wanted to stand behind him, protect him, and make sure he was okay. Since his return from Colorado, it was obvious things weren't okay with him. Things had changed. The trauma he had experienced there with the fires and the death of his close friends...that wasn't something a person could get over on their own and she highly doubted he was seeking therapy or other ways to cope, aside from alcohol.

But the old saying had held true still to this day. You can't help someone who refuses to help themselves. And Conner Jacobsen was the epitome for that phrase. He refused to allow anyone to help anyway, but even if he had, he wasn't doing much to help himself out of the mess of his past and the conflict of the present. So far, his future was uncertain and he couldn't care less.

"Hey."

His voice was soft behind her, quiet and unstartling. She turned to meet his eyes and couldn't help feeling sorry for him. He'd had a hell of a week and had a close call with a detrimental mistake with that dang battery cable and airbag. Part of this job, helping others while maintaining safety, offered no tolerance for mistakes. Life and death—the balance between the two weighed heavy on every call. Every step and action, reaction, and outcome meticulously planned and executed. Without a plan was a hasty decision and an action awaiting failure. The risk was far greater in this career than most would assume.

"Hey." The awkward silence between them hung thick in the air. She hated the fact work was getting the best of them and their friendship. His decisions and careless behavior were to blame. Work had nothing to do with it. They would be fine if he would get his head out of his ass and focus on doing the job and doing it well.

"Are we okay?" His question was full of concern as he stepped closer in order to lean against the truck. He had to know what he did on scene was not okay. He had to know he could have gotten someone seriously injured. Being forgetful on the job wasn't something taken lightly. But their friendship had withstood several years and small arguments, and she wasn't about to let this cause more friction between them.

She sighed, weighing her words carefully before speaking them. "Look, Con, you have to know we'll always be okay, but you have to pay attention. You can't waltz on scene and act like you know it all."

His brows furrowed, but he stayed quiet.

"You can't forget things either," she added, knowing he wouldn't stay quiet much longer.

"Meg, it's not like I forgot on purpose," he explained, grabbing a seat on the step of the truck. When he looked up, his eyes were filled with so much emotion, Megan had a hard time deciphering what he was truly feeling—somewhere between disappointment, anger, and frustration.

"No one forgets on purpose," she assured him, thankful he was remaining calm. "I just want to make sure your head is where it needs to be."

"Now you sound like my brother," he said in a huff. She couldn't blame him for being upset with his brother. The disagreements between those two dated far back to teen years for Conner, and there wasn't a hopeful end in sight. "Always telling me what I should and shouldn't do. Like you guys don't see me trying to make things right."

She nodded, thinking on what to say next because she knew this was delicate territory. His family had a past of disagreements and misunderstandings. Hell, there wasn't one family in this town she could think of who didn't. But Conner and Adam had never seen eye to eye, and part of that was blamed on the age difference between them. Add their father and his own judgments into the equation and it was a future World War III.

"I see you, Conner," Megan said, making sure he heard her. "But I also see Adam, and I saw the careless behavior on that scene, too."

"Careless behavior?" His face twisted in anger as he pushed off the step to stand in front of her. "Is that what you really think? I'm careless?"

She had said too much. She had always felt safe talking to him, but she should have known with everything happening, right now wasn't a good time to discuss the events of the scene and how she truly felt. But then again, the can of worms had been opened and there was no going back to having the elephant in the room with them.

"Megan, answer me," he said, reaching out to grab her

from her thoughts. "Is that what you really think? That I'm some smartass who doesn't give a shit about anything?"

She stood still, silently gauging his reaction, contemplating on how to calm him down and settle this without making things worse. She was a peace maker. She hated confrontation and she especially hated fighting with him.

"Answer me, Megan," he said, inching closer to her, invading her space until she looked at him and met his eyes with hers. "You think I don't care? That I'm going out of my way to purposely mess things up?"

"No," she said, the word barely escaping her lips in a whisper. "I don't think you're doing anything on purpose. I just..."

"Just what?" he asked, running a stressed hand through his hair. "You have no idea the amount of shit I've been through and how many lives depended on me. You have no idea what that's like, do you?"

Taken aback by his thoughtless assumption, she quickly counted to ten and tried her best to ignore it. But anger got the best of her. "Excuse me? What the hell is that supposed to mean?"

He tried to walk away. He tried to shrug her off, but this had gone too far and she wasn't allowing him the option to walk off and pretend he was right. "Where are you going? You don't get to run your mouth and walk away like that."

He turned, staring her down as she approached him.

"You don't get to say that kind of shit to me and walk away," she said, demanding he stay put and hear what she was about to say. "You have no idea what kind of shit I've been through in the last two years. You have no idea because you skipped off to Colorado to fight those *big* fires while I stayed here and dealt with everything on my own!

Don't tell me what I have and haven't been through! You don't have a clue!"

Silence. Like death between their friendship haunted the space between them as they stood only a few feet apart. His face was full of anger. Her heart full of pain and betrayal.

"Tell me," Conner said, taking a step in her direction. The pitiful look on his face as he realized how bad his words had hurt her made her question everything. "Please, tell me."

She shook her head and crossed her arms, taking a step back away from him, adding distance between them. "No. You tell me," she said, anger pulsing through her veins. "If you were so great at chasing big fires out in Colorado, why the hell did you come back here?"

Regret washed over his face as he looked in her direction before shrugging his shoulders. "I don't know."

And without anything else being said, he turned his back toward her and she had no choice but to let him walk away.

5

Driving away from the fire station, he couldn't help but think Megan had a point. If he was as good at fighting fires as he thought he was, why had he run from Colorado? From the opportunities he had been given when leaving Cedar Valley had seemed to be his only option. The escape from the small town life had given him a handful of regret and unstable outcomes. He had lost a few good friends to the forest fires in Colorado, but losing them couldn't compare to losing Megan.

Pulling into Granny Mae's Café, he parked the truck out front and killed the engine. He was still on call, but after what just went down at the station, he needed a break from the chaos and he would find his calm while grabbing a bite to eat.

Climbing out of the truck, he made his way to the door and pushed through it. Greeted by the bell above and a few friendly waves at the counter, Conner offered a wave back as he walked to an empty booth in the back. Out of sight and out of mind was where he wanted to be, but this small town saw everyone and everything. There was no hiding here in Cedar Valley.

"What can I get you to drink?" Granny Mae asked as she moseyed up to his booth. "You look like you could use a stronger drink than what I have to offer here, son."

A grin tugged at his lip and he couldn't help nodding in agreeance with her. He definitely needed something stronger than a Pepsi, but it was a no go as long as he was on duty. As much as he wanted to call it quits and head to Levy's, he wasn't a quitter and he never would be either.

"Rough day already?" Granny Mae asked, tapping her FitBit on her wrist to check the time. And here he thought only younger people had the damn things attached to their wrists. Another thought crossed his mind, making him wonder what an older lady like her would need a FitBit for.

Shaking his head to clear the random thoughts, he said, "Yeah, I guess you can say that."

"Well, let me get you a cold Pepsi and I'll be right back to take your order," Granny Mae said, spinning on her heels, and clacked her way back to the counter.

He couldn't brush off the feeling of someone eyeing him from across the way. He looked over his shoulder and met eyes with Rosie, Megan's grandmother. The look of concern she gave him told him everything he needed to know. She wasn't thrilled about his return to Cedar Valley, and that meant she wasn't thrilled about him with Megan either.

He was sure word had spread like wildfire through this town, and was even more sure Rosie had heard of his forgetfulness on the last call. He knew she hadn't wanted Megan to join the squad. According to Megan, Rosie swore chasing fires was an invitation for an early funeral. He could only imagine what thoughts were racing through Rosie's head when she realized her granddaughter ran calls with him—a forgetful know-it-all who only cared about himself. No matter how hard he argued against that label, he knew his actions spoke louder. He had never been a selfish person. Hell, he was a firefighter, for Pete's sake. He wanted to help people. Rescue them from their bad days and save them from hell when hell became too much to handle. Since coming back, it seemed he was only making things worse, and he wasn't doing a good enough job proving his worth to the service, or this town.

He nodded with a friendly wave in Rosie's direction, but she looked down and away as if she wasn't studying him for the last few minutes. "Don't worry, Rose, I hear you loud and clear," he mumbled as Granny Mae arrived with his drink and a notepad ready to take his order.

"Don't you worry about her, son," Granny Mae said, hitching a thumb back in the direction Rosie had been standing. "She's just looking out for her granddaughter. There are no hard feelings or anything to take personal, ya hear? This town's glad to have you back and there isn't a darn thing you could do to change that."

He wasn't sure about that. Maybe Granny needed an update on the latest happenings at the station. Maybe then she would recant her statement and tell him to think twice about what he was doing back in this town.

"What are you thinkin' of havin' to eat?" Granny Mae asked, flipping the menu open to the daily specials. "We've got your favorite biscuits and gravy. Or how about the *Hungry Man* special?"

He leaned in for a closer look, catching a glimpse of all that was included in the *Hungry Man* platter when she flipped the menu shut and folded it in the crook of her arm.

"That's what I'll make you. A nice round plate full of eggs, bacon, sausage, hash browns, and your choice of toast or pancakes?"

It wasn't a question, but more of a statement. She had already made her mind up and he didn't have a choice in the matter. Unless of course, he didn't want toast, then he could have pancakes. Where the heck did she think all that food would go? Not that he was in perfect shape, but he liked to think he'd been working on a six pack for the last six months—even if they weren't yet too defined to notice.

"Toast or pancakes?" she asked, making it clear this was his choice and time was ticking.

"Toast, please," he said, reaching for his glass to take a drink.

"White or wheat?"

"I have a choice in that too?" He couldn't believe the options he was given at a restaurant. Endless possibilities meant a full stomach. More than full—stuffed was more like it. "I'll take wheat, thank you."

Flipping her notepad shut, she crammed the mini thing into the overfull pocket of her apron. "I'll get that right out to you. Don't you be running off until you eat, ya hear?"

Nodding, he grabbed his glass again. He couldn't make any promises, but if it meant something, he didn't want to leave here without eating. The food smelled delicious and he had the rest of the day ahead of him. The only thing he needed now was a cup of coffee. Except he didn't drink it. Coffee would be the last thing he ever drank to make it through a day around here. The last time he tried coffee came to mind and he couldn't help shake off the nasty bitter taste the memory caused in his mouth. Scrunching his nose, he dug into his pocket and pulled out his phone.

No missed calls. No text messages. A blank screen peered back at him and he couldn't help but think about Megan and the hurtful things he had said. That she had said. They had attacked each other for what? To prove a point about how careless he had been acting. Hell, she had been telling the truth and he was dumb enough to argue with her about it. Sometimes the truth hurt, and sometimes —scratch that, most of the time, he couldn't handle it. He was definitely his father's son.

Leaving the café after overstuffing his belly full of Granny's delicious food, Conner had plenty of time to ponder over the ways he would apologize and make things right with Megan. Her ability to suppress anger impressed him. Her being Irish had nothing on her when it came to her temperament and ability to control her anger.

Regardless of her abilities when it came to anger management, what he said had been wrong, and he realized she only said the things she had because he had hurt her first. The last thing he wanted was to hurt her. She had been there for him through thick and thin. They had been there for each other through everything. Her parents' divorce. His father's inability to accept him like he had Adam. Her mother's death from cancer. And even over the last two years, he knew she had his back as he fought fires in Colorado. He had lost touch with her over those two long years, but that didn't mean he quit caring. Getting caught up in life was to blame. Nothing could take his focus entirely away from the one thing he cared the most about in Cedar Valley.

Pulling his truck into an empty parking space next to

the station, he shifted into park and killed the engine. He hoped by the time he made his way inside, Megan would be cooled off and ready for him to apologize for acting selfish and inconsiderate. Whether she would accept his apology was another worry altogether.

Hopping out of the truck, he slammed the door and made his way to the open bay door. Megan was nowhere in sight when he first walked in. He found Adam wiping down the kitchen counter, cleaning up after midmorning breakfast.

"Hey, where's Megan?" he asked, not caring if he drew attention to his need to find her.

Adam looked over his shoulder. "She's not with you?"

Conner shook his head. If only things hadn't turned out the way they had hours ago, they would have most likely eaten breakfast together and caught up in the latest happenings in each other's lives. He had blown that, though, and now Megan wasn't here.

"I haven't seen her. I thought she had gone with you to the café or something," Adam said, finishing wiping off the stove, and made a stack of dishes in the sink. "You sure she isn't around here somewhere?"

The station wasn't massive in size. There was no extra space a person could escape to without being seen by at least one other person. The bedrooms were connected by a long, drawn out hallway leading to the kitchen and lounge area with a television and Xbox. Not forgetting the training room and fitness center. If she was hanging around here, she would have been seen by now.

Adam shrugged. "Maybe she went to Rosie's?"

Conner shook his head. "Nah, Rosie's working at the café today. I just saw her a while ago."

Adam tossed the rag into the sink and turned his attention back to Conner. "What's up?"

Conner hated when his brother read him like a book. His brother had ten years on him and was far too mature for being in his early thirties. But, being young and immature, Conner looked up to Adam because he had everything going for him in this life—a house, a soon-to-be wife, two amazing children, and he was fire chief in this small town. He was completely set to live comfortably for the rest of his life until retirement. Conner, on the other hand, didn't even have his own place to live. He lived with Adam and felt more and more like a mooch each passing day.

"Hey, I know things have gotten off to a bad start around here, but you've gotta understand it's nothing personal, okay?"

"Yeah, of course," Conner said, waving him off as he made his way toward the garage. "Nothing personal."

"Hey," Adam called after him. "I mean it."

Conner nodded and was almost out of the kitchen when the tones dropped. His pager squawked and vibrated against his leg as dispatch alerted all units were needed for a structure fire in the outskirts of town. "All units be advised unknown occupancy at this time. Deputies are contacting home owners. I repeat, unknown occupancy at this time."

Shrugging into his turnout gear, Conner shoved his feet into his boots as he yanked his coat off a nearby hook along with his helmet.

Climbing into the rig's driver seat, he saw the top of a strawberry blonde's head bob around the front end of the truck and climb into the passenger seat next to him. She was still pissed, but at least she glanced over at him, acknowledging his presence.

He waited for the rest of the squad to climb aboard before pulling out of the garage.

"The Rickeys live at that address," Megan shouted over the sirens. "They've got a house full of animals, a couple cats, a couple dogs, and a couple of young kids."

The thought of the young kids being home alone crossed Conner's mind. It had been a while since he had responded to a call involving kids. Kids made for tough calls. The last call he had involving a kid didn't end well and left him with months full of therapy sessions. He hoped this call wasn't a case like that. He wasn't ready to add it to the top of his endless pile of shit.

Dark, gray smoke billowed out of the house and became increasingly thicker once he rolled the truck onto the scene. The flames flickered angry spats against the outline of busted out windows. Red hot and no match for anyone without gear on. Looking at Megan, he nodded as he climbed down from the driver's seat.

They hadn't been on too many fire calls together, but for a moment, he felt connected to her and knew they would be just fine with this one.

Hollering over the shouts on scene, he saw Adam pull up behind the rig in the department's SUV. Fire Chief to the rescue was all he could think when he saw his brother behind the wheel. It'd make their father proud to know Adam was so loyally respondent on these calls.

Shrugging off his envy, he grabbed an axe and hoisted a hose over his shoulder. He shouted to the newbie to crank the water full blast and jogged toward the house. He was on a mission to fight this fire and prove he was worthy enough to be here in Cedar Valley. To prove he could handle his job and do it right. He would prove that to Adam, to Megan, and to anyone else who needed proving to.

He looked back one last time at Megan, who was busy rounding up the necessary tools for the job. She was good at what she did. He knew that, she knew that, hell, the whole town knew that. She didn't need him telling her what she could and couldn't handle. Hell, she could probably teach him a thing or two.

Planting his feet firmly on the ground, he opened the valve and allowed the water to race out as he aimed it low and steady at the flickering flames. The amount of chaos on a fire call was intense and more than insane. Adrenaline hummed through his veins, pulsed in his heart, and deafened his ears, but he was still able to hear a cry for help when there was one.

Cranking the valve shut on his hose, he dropped it and turned back to his crew. They hadn't heard it like he had, but if they had, they would be making their way in there, doing something, anything, to save whoever that voice belonged to.

"Adam!" he shouted in a desperate plea for his brother to hear him. "There's a kid in there! I'm going in!"

The last words he heard before racing to the open door of the flame-filled house belonged to Adam telling him to stand down and stay outside. The house was unsafe. There was no way to make it out once he was in. But those words meant nothing as he raced inside, determined to find the child who was crying for their help. This was his opportunity to prove he was worthy enough to stay in Cedar Valley and that he was able to do his job right.

He would prove it to everyone that he was determined enough to become the best firefighter Cedar Valley ever saw. But first, he had to make his way in and rescue this kid. There was no time to kill as he hustled into the fully engulfed house in search of the voice calling for help in the thickest clouds of smoke and hottest of flames.

Risking his own life, he would find this child and bring them to safety.

Boards fell, flames flashed nearby, and in his peripheral vision, he saw his safe escape narrowing further with every step he took inside the house.

6

Radio static and muffled shouts were heard as he made his way in the direction of the crying and screaming. Adrenaline coursed through his blood, making him well aware of his surroundings, but he refused to back down from finding the trapped kid. He had nieces and nephews. He wouldn't leave them in the balance of death, so there would be no way he would leave this child to a fiery hell.

Smoke blurred his vision, making it difficult to see more than two feet in front of him. Boards collapsed behind him as he focused on his mission to make it to the back of the house. The only part of the house that had yet to catch fire. He prayed the kid was low enough on the floor in order to get all the oxygen they could get until Conner could find them.

The thought of being too late crossed his mind once the shouting suppressed to muffled cries. "Fire department! Call out!" he shouted, anger and panic overwhelming his voice as he trampled his way to the far back corner of the house. "Call out!"

The subtle scream of a child who couldn't be no older than his nephew, Tyler, was heard from the direction of a closed door that greeted Conner on his way down the dark hallway. Wasting no time, he busted through the hollow door hindering his rescue.

There in the corner sat a trembling boy with tears streaming down his face as he cried and coughed with each breath inhaled. Conner grabbed his radio from his shoulder and yelled, "I need everyone on the southeast corner of the house! Now! I've got one coming out!"

He reached out to the child, offering a steady hand for the child to grab onto. Trying hard to maintain control of his emotions, his adrenaline, and everything in between, Conner talked slow and calm to the child. "What's your name?"

"Sammy," the boy whispered between subtle coughs. His airway was most likely irritated by smoke inhalation while waiting for Conner to rescue him.

"Okay, Sammy, my name's Conner and I'm going to get you out of here, okay?"

The little boy nodded and took hold of Conner's hand. Shoving aside the emotions in order to focus on the job was Conner's specialty, but even now he had to admit this shit was hard to do.

"Okay, Sammy, I have to find a way for us to get out," he said, turning back to the scared boy who was placing a whole helluva lot of trust in Conner right now. Covering the boy's face with his mask, he told the boy to hold it to his face and keep it there. Before leaving the room, he said, "Stay right here for just a minute, okay? I'll be right back."

When the boy nodded, Conner turned back to the path he abandoned and made it out into the hallway he entered the room from. Nothing but black smoke and flames could be seen. The flames had jumped from one area of the house to their area in a matter of minutes. There was no exit the way he had come in and there was definitely no exit out the back of the house as it was being guarded by the intense flames he had fought to get to where he was now.

Turning back to face the boy, he faced the truth of the situation—he had messed up. He didn't have a backup plan. He should have never crossed the threshold of the front door until given the okay. Now, because he didn't wait, he had to face the consequences.

Refusing to let them die, he found his way across the room. There had to be a window somewhere along the outside wall.

Fumbling around in the dark, trying hard to hold his breath as he made his way to the window, Conner held tight to a little hand that was counting on him to get them out of this mess. He refused to give up. He would not give up. He would die trying.

"Sammy, keep that mask on your face, okay, bud?"

Sammy nodded as he held the oversized oxygen mask against his face. Conner made sure the boy was protected from breaking glass before shattering the window he stumbled against. He prayed like hell the crew were standing right outside, ready for the boy in his arms.

It was hard to swallow, hard to breathe. He needed to get this boy out and then pull himself out the window. Once he could do that, all would be good. He wouldn't need to worry any longer. The boy would be safe—they would be safe.

Adam greeted him on the other side of the shattered window. Clearing the jagged pieces, Adam pulled the boy from Conner's arms and handed him off to the medics on scene. They were ready and willing to do whatever they had to do to save the little boy's life.

Conner tried to make it out the window, but his foot caught on his way up, causing him to fall back as he jerked and thrashed his leg to untangle the mess that was keeping him back. Blankets and bedsheets wrapped around his legs as he plummeted to the floor. *Dammit.* He had made it this far. Why the hell was this happening to him?

Adam's voice shouted in at him over the sound of more breaking glass and the staticky traffic on the handheld radio at his side. "Get up! Get over here now!"

Conner kicked and thrashed, trying his hardest to untangle the mass of bedding at his feet. It was no use. His lungs hurt, his head was pounding, and he was suffocating—plain and simple, he was going to die.

Growling, he attempted to force himself up off the floor and in the direction of the window. Megan's voice called out to him, screaming at the top of her lungs as she rushed to his side. He had no idea how she got in there, but he was thankful she had. There was nothing more embarrassing than needing someone to rescue the rescuer. He was glad it was her and not Adam. Wherever the hell Adam was, he couldn't believe the son of a bitch wasn't in here getting him out.

"Conner, let's go! Get up!" she shouted in his face, yanking him to his feet after clearing the pile of blankets and rubble from his feet. He leaned against her, weak and more than willing to give up now. "Walk, Conner! Move!"

Flames flashed behind them, taunting their safety as they made their way to the window. With everything he had left in him, Conner climbed with Megan's help into the open frame of a busted out window and fell into Adam's arms. Adam carried him to a nearby ambulance cot and set him down.

"Megan," he tried saying, his throat full of sandpaper.

"Relax, she's out," the medic said, pressing Conner back against the cot in order to get the oxygen mask on his face. "You're one lucky son of a bitch, you know that?"

"Where's Sammy?" Conner asked, refusing to listen to the medic's bullshit. He only cared about the kid. Nothing else mattered at the moment.

"Who?"

"The kid!" Conner sat up but was pressed back into the cot by the asshole medic. "Where's he at?"

"You need to chill out, dude. He's already on his way to the hospital," the medic said, pressing the oxygen mask tightly against Conner's face. Conner gave up. He relaxed. The kid was safe. He was safe.

Megan. She was safe, but dammit if he didn't want to kick her ass for risking her life to save him. He would have to face the wrath he was sure would come. She would most likely kick his ass first—that was unless Adam beat her to it.

7

Standing on scene, hearing Adam tell Conner to stand down, watching Conner ignore Adam's command and run into the fully engulfed house without thinking twice had done a number on her. The emotions from that scene were enough to make her want to puke.

As a medic, she had been on several bad calls. Bad calls with horrible scenes, but none involving a kid in a fire, trapped and screaming for someone to save them from the inescapable disaster. Her heart had caught in her throat. Her stomach had done a double flip and knotted inside out.

Seeing Conner run into that house and realizing he might not make it back out caused her to act without thinking it through. At that exact moment, all of her senses had left her and the only thought she had was to go in after him—to help him, to be there to bring him out just in case...

"Hey, I want to talk to you about what happened back there," Adam said, motioning for her to follow him into his office as he shut the door behind her when she entered, taking a chair across the desk from his seat.

She watched him walk around to his side of the desk,

keeping an eye on his facial expressions. She knew this wasn't going to be a good conversation, but in all honesty, she also knew she deserved whatever punishment from the book Adam wanted to throw at her.

"What happened back there?"

The question was loaded. She knew exactly what he was wanting to hear, but for some reason, she couldn't come up with the words to tell him. There was a reason she ran in after Conner. The reason wasn't as simple as *he's my partner*. And it sure wasn't simple to explain anything she had felt while on scene, watching chaos unfold right at their fingertips.

"Okay," he said, straightening in his chair as he pulled up closer to the desk in order to lean forward onto his elbows. "I know you and Conner have a friendship. I also know you are one helluva paramedic, and now a firefighter."

"But?" In cases like these, there was always a *but* and she had a feeling she already knew what that *but* entailed.

"But...it's my job to make sure we all go home safe every night after our shift," he said, keeping his eyes on her, waiting for her to agree with him—which she did—more than did.

She knew the dangers of the job. She knew what it took to be responsible for everyone while losing control of everything else. She knew. Within minutes, a person's fate could change and before long, they were lost in the chaos and the blame got pushed back on the lead. She'd been there, done that. Several times.

"Megan, I can't have you getting your emotions mixed up with doing your job," he said, making it obvious he knew exactly what had happened on scene. "Like I said, you're one helluva medic and firefighter. You've got what a lot of people don't—determination to do your job and to do it well."

"But?"

"But, I can't have emotions or feelings getting in the way of doing the best job we can while on scene. I know, you handle them well, but today, while on that call, I saw the look on your face before you ran in after my brother."

She could only imagine what her face looked like in that exact moment, but clearly, it was obvious enough for Adam to call her out on it. She nodded. There were yet no words to explain to him what had gone through her mind, or what the hell had made her chase after him when every bit of common sense and training told her to stay put. To stand down and do nothing but what she was trained to do—spray water and fight the fire. She knew why she didn't. She knew and so did Adam. He knew exactly what she wasn't saying.

"I should suspend you," he said, leaning back in his chair as he kept his eyes focused on her reaction, but she didn't react. She had known it would come. The logical part of her brain, the same one that had malfunctioned in telling her to stay put and not run into the fully engulfed house, had realized it messed up and with mistakes came consequences. Before she could follow up his statement with a questionable "but," he said, "But I'm not. I'm letting you off the hook with a verbal warning. The next time...no, there won't be a next time."

He pushed back his chair and she followed suit. The knock at the door interrupted the final words and she was thankful. She wanted nothing more than to run and hide, and eat a pint of ice cream while watching reruns of *Chicago Fire*.

Except when Adam opened the door to let her out of his office, she came face-to-face with the one who got her in this position in the first place. Furrowing her brow, she did a double take on her way by. "What are you doing here? Aren't you supposed to be in the hospital?"

He shrugged and she hated how smug he was in a time like this. "I left."

"You left?" Adam questioned, leaning against the doorframe. "What do you mean you left?"

Another shrug, followed by that shit-eating grin of his. "I left. Signed AMA and walked out of the hospital."

She couldn't believe what he was saying. Although, every patient had the right to refuse care, sign the form, and leave on their own, Conner had taken the brunt of the fire when he was stuck in that bedroom. The smoke had been so thick, she hadn't been able to see her own gloved hand in front of her face.

"I'm fine," Conner said, keeping his focus on her. "There's not a lot that'll keep me down for long."

"You're so full of yourself, you know that?" She turned to leave, but Adam had the final word this time as he told Conner to get in his office. She should have walked away, but instead, she watched the aftermath of Conner's insubordination bite him in the ass.

"What the hell were you thinking running into that damn house?" Adam hollered, his tone fierce and intimidating. Thankfully, he hadn't used that with her, or she would have been a sobbing mess in that chair Conner was now sitting in. Conner stayed quiet, leaning back without a single reaction to anything his brother had just asked him. "Are you trying to get yourself killed? Huh? Are you really that convinced you know what you're doing that you don't listen to my commands on scene? Do you have any idea how lucky you are right now?"

Another shrug, making her want to reach in there and

slap him silly. She couldn't believe what she was witnessing. A part of her knew the stubbornness of the Jacobsens and the other knew Conner wasn't the same person he had been when he left town two years ago.

"It's not about luck," he finally said, and Megan felt her gut twist. She shouldn't be standing here to witness this train wreck, but she couldn't make herself leave either. She needed to be there and to hear everything Conner had been thinking when he ignored Adam's command and took it upon himself to be the hero of the day. "I had a job to do and I did it."

Adam slammed his hand down on the desk. Papers scattered, flipping off the edge of the desk and onto the floor. Megan jumped, but Conner had no reaction. He sat still, waiting silently for the other shoe to drop. And that shoe was going to drop any minute. "I'm pretty sure the key word there is *had*," Adam said, standing over Conner, a fierce look on his face. She watched in silence, holding her breath and praying they wouldn't battle this out right here in the office.

Conner stood, knocking the chair back out of the way, and stood toe to toe with Adam. "What are you going to do, huh? Let me go?" he shouted, spitting words in Adam's face.

Adam didn't flinch, but instead remained silent as his brother shouted obscenities an inch from his face.

"Huh? Is that what you want to do? You're pissed because I actually did my job, what I was trained to actually fucking do and ran into that house to save that kid? You're pissed because you didn't have the balls to and I did? For once—"

The words vanished, the breath knocked out of Conner when Adam slammed him onto the corner of the desk. "You have no idea what the hell you're talking about, and you sure as hell don't have the common sense to know the difference."

Adam slammed a pointed finger into Conner's chest. "I should let you go. I should kick you off this service and never let you back on."

"There are a lot of things you *should* do, but what you should've done is helped me save that fucking kid!"

"Why? So both of us could've taken the risk of losing our lives?" Adam's voice was a near shout, filled with anger and a rasp from yelling. "What the hell do you think that would do to Mom and Dad? Losing us both."

"This isn't about them," Conner said, pushing back against Adam as he made his way off the edge of the desk. "This isn't about anything you're making it about. I saved a kid's life, man. A kid around the same age as Tyler. What the hell was I supposed to do? Let that kid cry and burn up in that damn house?"

Megan felt her heart skip several beats. Sweat formed at the thought of the possibility of losing not only the kid, but Conner too. And not to mention her own life.

Adam's face twisted as though he was thinking Conner had a point, but conflicted with what was right according to policy and what was morally correct.

Megan should've never stayed to watch this unfold. Both brothers were backing down, while her heart raced. Fight or flight had never been this strong before. "He's right, you know?" she said, taking Conner's side in this argument. Knowing, once again, she was crossing the line—a fine line at that.

Adam held his hand up, attempting to keep her in the distance, a signal she refused to pay any attention to as she continued to step into the office. "That kid could have been Tyler, and then what?"

Adam shook his head, pointing a finger in her direction. "No, you don't get to use my son as a stance in justifying yours and Conner's actions. What you two did on scene today was complete bullshit and you know it. There's no way to justify ignoring my commands just to save someone from a fully engulfed house. Listen to that one more time," he said, holding up a finger to keep them quiet. "A fully engulfed house. A trap. One you both are lucky you escaped alive from. What the hell am I supposed to do with you two?"

It was her turn to shrug. She was all out of answers for herself, let alone his questions too. She knew the wrath of Rosie was going to come soon too, and she hated the thought of making her grandmother worry so much. It was bad enough her grandmother hadn't wanted her to join the fire department, but now, there was no question about it. Her grandmother would be calling her soon enough, confronting her head-on to find out what in the ever-loving hell she could have possibly been thinking when she ran into the death trap of a house.

The ringing of her phone interrupted the tension in the room. Of course, it would be her phone ringing, *and* it would be her grandmother. Karma must really hate her today. Before she could decide whether to answer the call or not, Conner shoved past her and left the office before either of them had time to tell him to wait.

8

Leaving the office was something he had no choice but to do. He hated the fact Megan was putting her neck on the line to save him and his job. She had every right to stand up for him, but it wasn't what he wanted her to do. She risked her life coming in after him on scene today, and now, she was risking suspension or worse.

He already knew his brother was dead serious about letting him go. Adam wouldn't hesitate too long about it. If he wanted Conner gone, he'd be out without a doubt. The fact he was back in Cedar Valley, running from the last two years in Colorado, he wanted to make things right. He wanted so bad to prove he was wise enough to stick around and mature enough to have what others had.

Instead, he was messing it all up. It had been wrong of him to justify running into that house with saving a kid, but he couldn't care less. Sometimes, acting on morals and beliefs was much better than acting on principle alone. The policy handbook didn't care about morals. It cared about black and white. It left no room for gray, and in this profession, there was a helluva lot of gray area. This job wasn't some simple black and white decision. Every call involved making a last-minute decision and this time, he had made a decision that had everyone guessing his senses.

To hell with it, he would figure it out in the morning. He hollered at the newbie on the way out, asking him to cover the last hour of his shift. Another ding against him more than likely, but right now, a good stiff drink was calling his name and he wasn't going to ignore it.

Pulling his truck into the back parking lot of Levy's, he made sure he hid it out of sight from anyone watching his every move—like his brother or Megan. He wanted peace and quiet tonight. Having a few drinks never hurt anyone and if they begged to differ, he would set them straight.

Swinging the door open, he was met by the smell of strong perfume and smoke. Not a good combination, but on a night like tonight, he didn't care. He walked in, nodding at several people who turned to see who had just entered through the back door. He made his way straight for the counter. He wanted a straight shot of Tequila or two, and who knew what else.

"Where's Megan?" Liam asked, leaving one customer's side after refilling their drink.

Conner couldn't believe this. How the hell was he supposed to know where Megan was? Why the hell would Liam ask him that for?

"You're asking me?" Conner asked, pointing a finger into his chest as he glanced around him. Sure, he felt cocky tonight, but in all honesty, why the hell would Liam ask him about Megan?

Liam reached for a glass and filled it with the next mix on the list for a customer sitting beside Conner. "You two were on that call today, right? I just figured you two would be hanging out after the shift."

Conner nodded before pointing to the bottle of tequila behind Liam. "I'll take a double shot of that."

Liam turned, looking back in the direction Conner had pointed. He turned his head back to Conner and asked, "Are you sure about that? Do you remember the last time you had tequila?"

Yeah, he sure remembered all right. How could he forget? He had made the biggest fool out of himself, but that was neither here nor there. "Just get me a double shot. I'll keep my cool this round, I promise."

"All right, but only because I know you've had a shit day," Liam said, reaching back to pull the bottle of tequila out of its spot. He poured the shots, lining them up in front of Conner.

"Shit day is an understatement," Conner said, tossing back the first shot before quickly tossing back the second. "And it isn't even over yet."

Instead of venting it out with Liam, who had other things to concern himself with, like making his customers happy, Conner ventured over to a nearby table full of women he'd never seen before. If he was going to fail professionally, he might as well fail all the way around. One-night stands weren't his thing anymore, but tonight, he could make do with a wild round or two between the sheets.

"You ladies from around here?" he asked, moseying his way into a chair at their table. They had the perfect spot, right next to the jukebox. He would make his way over to it just after pleasantries. He wanted to make sure these women weren't from around here before he wasted his time talking to them.

"No, we're here on vacation," the blonde said, giggling like she was in high school.

"Vacation? Here?" he asked, pointing at the table. "What brought you here?"

"Our uncle," the brunette said, looking grumpier by the minute. Obviously, Conner wasn't the only one not wanting to be stuck in this town.

"Oh yeah? Who's your uncle?" He only asked to make sure they wouldn't be able to find out who he was in the morning after their quick romp in the sheets.

"Tom Richards."

He hadn't heard that name before. There weren't any Richards from around here as far as he knew. "He live here?"

The blonde shook her head. "No, he's here on a business call," she said between hiccups. "He's hauling some cattle back with us that he's buying from Wes Spencer."

There went the idea of having fun with a woman no one knew around here. The last thing he needed was a trail to link him back to this night and his unbalanced decision-making skills.

"Do you know Wes?" the blonde asked, taking another drink even though it was quite obvious she should stop while she was ahead.

"Yeah, I do," Conner answered her innocent question. "Everyone knows Wes around here, but he's my gramps' best friend."

"Aww, that sounds so sweet," the blonde said, batting her eyelashes in his direction. She was not his type—not at all. She was wasting her time trying to get him to pay more attention to her, especially when the brunette sitting next to her rolled her eyes and acted less impressed with this conversation than Conner.

"What do you do?" the blonde asked, failing to realize Conner was no longer interested in her or her friend.

"I'm a firefighter," he answered, knowing most women he said this to turned into goo and swooned over him. Instant gratification of being a firefighter. Women loved hunky firefighters, and even though he hadn't been focused on working out in the last couple of months, he would like to think of himself as one of those hunky firefighters women hoped would show up to rescue kittens from their trees. "Well, I was...or whatever."

His eye caught a glimpse of a strawberry blonde coming through the front entrance of the bar. Levy's was a public place, and he was the last person to decide who came and who stayed, but the last person he wanted to see was her.

"Look, it's been fun talking with you, ladies, but I gotta go," he said, tapping the table before stepping away. If luck was still on his side, he could make it to the back exit without Megan finding him among the weeknight crowd.

"Do you have a number?" the brunette asked, reaching into her purse to pull out her phone. The most words he heard that woman say in the last thirty minutes.

He shook his head and headed for the exit, hoping he would make it to the door in time and the two women at the table would forget they had a conversation with him.

He slapped a twenty on the counter, told Liam to keep the change, and continued on his mission to the back door he had entered not too long ago. He had lost sight of Megan among the shuffle between people on the way to the counter. He could only hope he could make it out of here without her finding him.

Seven steps from the exit and he heard his name being

called from somewhere behind him. Part of him fought to turn around, focus on her for the night, and try to make things right once again, but the part that would most likely win couldn't care about anything right now. He had messed up a lot lately. It had pissed a lot of people off, but the last two he wanted to piss off was the girl who had been his best friend for the last twenty some years and his brother. And now, his best friend was walking up to him, her eyes locked on his as she made her way over.

He could have made it out of there. He could have made a quick run for it, but there was something from the look in her eyes telling him not to leave. Not to run. For the first time in his life, he fought against running and stayed put.

"Hey, where are you going? I just got here. I've been looking for you," she said, and it took everything for him to pull it together to tell her something, anything, to squash her concern over him.

He pulled at his shirt collar, feeling a sudden rush of heat creep up his neck into his face. Something about her was pulling his attention away from running. He didn't like the feeling. Something he had never felt before and vowed to never feel for his best friend. "I was just getting ready to call it a night and head home."

A little white lie considering the unfolding of events after today's call, but he had nothing else at the ready. Home wasn't home anymore. Home was staying with his brother, but now that he had crossed a line of no return, he thought it would be best not to go back to Adam's for a while—a long while.

9

Grabbing her pager and following Conner out of the fire department had seemed the right option at the time. Adam had hollered after her, telling her to "let him go," but she refused to listen on a personal level. It most likely pissed Adam off, but she didn't care enough to stay back and let the train wreck explode further.

Her first thought had been to check out Levy's, but for some reason, it had been the last place she stopped. Checking the café, Adam's house, and coming up empty-handed, she had pulled into Levy's parking lot.

His truck was nowhere in sight, but that didn't mean he hadn't ditched it or parked it out back. Climbing out of her car after taking the key out, she locked the doors and made her way inside. At first glance, the bar was crowded and a quick scan hadn't revealed what she came looking for.

Until she heard laughter coming from a table across the way with a cute blonde and a brunette, who were currently being entertained by none other than Conner Jacobsen—her prime target.

He must have caught a glance at her, because he

beelined it toward the back exit. She wasn't going to let him get away that easy. She wanted to talk to him. Their friendship deserved as much, unless, of course, their friendship was no longer valid...

"Hey, where are you going? I just got here. I've been looking all over town for you," she said, taking a hold of his arm to keep him from running out the door.

He pulled at his collar, his face turning red as his jaw tensed.

"I was just getting ready to call it a night and head home."

Short and sweet, to the point. He was pissed. Was he pissed she found him here? "Why don't we sit at the bar? We can talk over a few drinks?"

He wanted to tell her no. It was written all over his face. He wasn't interested in sitting down and having a conversation with her. It was obvious and it took everything she had to hide the hurt she felt by that observation.

He shrugged and ran a hand through his hair. "I guess."

He took a step away from the door and headed in the direction of open barstools at the counter. She followed him. She hated the distance between them. She hated it now more than ever that there wasn't an actual physical distance between them, but an emotional divide the size of the equator.

Sliding into an open spot, she looked over at Liam and asked for something strong. The day had been long, and the night would be even longer if she could get Conner to talk and they could go back to normal.

"What do you want to talk about?" His sarcasm dripped from every word he said before taking a shot, throwing it back quick with a chaser. "Did my brother send you to find me?"

"What? No," she said, offended he would think such a thing. If his brother wanted to find him, Adam would have gone looking himself. He wouldn't have sent her to do his dirty work. This train wreck had gotten completely blown apart and she wasn't sure if there would be any way to put the pieces back together. "I came on my own."

"That was nice of you," he said, chasing back another shot. "But I'm a big boy and can handle my own. I don't need anyone to help me through this."

Taken aback by his harsh words, she reached for her Jack and Coke and chugged it. She needed a drink to mellow out before she snapped on him. All feelings aside, he was a good firefighter. His heart was in it and Cedar Valley was lucky to have him on the department. But, feelings were tied in, and they would be when it came to what they'd shared and the friendship they'd held onto for so long now. It hurt to watch him act like she wasn't there at all as he slammed back shot after shot.

"Is that what you think?"

He turned, furrowed his brows, and said, "No, it's what I know. I don't need you, or him, or anyone for that matter."

"When did you become so damned bullheaded and rude?" Hiding the hurt with anger was her only option now. Either way, he wasn't paying attention to her, so it wouldn't matter if she bawled her eyes out while begging him to see what was at stake right in front of him.

"When did you become so concerned with what I'm doing?" He looked over his shoulder in the direction of the blonde's table before looking at her. "Things changed, Meg. I'm not the same person anymore."

Her eyes followed his gaze, looked at the blonde and back at him. She couldn't believe how senseless this whole situation had become. "I've always been concerned. I'm your best friend. I lo—" Biting her tongue, she quickly grabbed her glass and downed her drink in order to shut her mouth. There would be no way she would spill her feelings to him tonight. The mood he was in...

Slamming down his empty glass, he leaned forward on the counter and looked at her. She knew tears were welling in her eyes. She knew the dam was about to break. She also knew she shouldn't take this personal. He was going through a rough patch in life and regardless of what he said, he needed her, or anyone for that matter. So much was at stake, and she wasn't going to let him walk away again.

"Listen, Meg," he said, outlining the rim of his glass with his finger before giving the glass a shake, causing the ice to slosh around. He tipped it back, took an ice cube in his mouth, and crushed it between his teeth as he kept his eyes locked on hers. "I wanted to come here tonight to get away. I needed somewhere to go to be alone and so I came here. The last thing I expected was for you to follow me."

"Okay, but I did," she said, not understanding where he was taking this conversation. It wasn't like she was crowding him or keeping him here against his will. He could have left a long time ago. Granted, it would have pissed her off, possibly hurt her worse than the words he'd said tonight, but she would have had no choice but to let him go. "So, what's the big deal?"

Shaking his head, he held his empty glass up in the air and requested another mixed drink for both of them. He twisted in his spot, turning to face her. The mix of emotion crossed his face and she felt pained for him. Whatever he had experienced in Colorado, add in the conflict between his father and him, and now the conflict between him and Adam, it had him losing his mind.

"You shouldn't have," he said, keeping his eyes on her as

she waited impatiently for him to get the point he was trying to make. "You shouldn't have done what you did on scene today either. You should have let me go."

Shaking her head, she crossed her arms. She wasn't going to hear this from him. She knew damn well he would have done the same if it were the other way around. "You're my best friend, Conner. Don't tell me what I should've done. That's not the problem here."

"Well, now you've got problems because of me," Conner said, swiping a loose hair from his face. "The last thing you need is problems because of me. And that's what you've got now."

"Let me decide what I need," she said, her tongue sharp and her words striking a nerve in him. "I do what I want. I don't need anyone telling me different."

He chuckled as he brought the glass to his mouth. Pointing a finger at her, he said, "Now you've got my attitude and you know where I'm coming from. Yes?"

"No," she said, swearing this conversation wasn't getting anywhere. She hated the stubborn trait he inherited from his father. There was no talking to them when they had something confirmed in their brain. No proving them wrong either. And right now, Conner was wrong. "You're wanting to give up. You can't give up. You've got so much going for you here."

Full-on laughter escaped as he leaned his head back. She was glad he was finding this funny. "You think..." Another laugh. "You think I've got a lot going for me? Here?"

"Yes."

Shaking his head, he said, "You're wrong. I don't have anything here. I live in my brother's house, which if you remember, is in a pissing match with me. And my father hates my guts. I was a firefighter, but now Adam wants to take that from me, too."

"He doesn't want to take anything from you," she tried to explain, but he wasn't having it.

"That house wasn't good for me anyway. Too much talk about wedding stuff and it was making me sick," he said, tossing back the rest of his drink. "He'd be doing me a favor if he kicked me off the service. I'm out of his house now anyway, but now I have nowhere to stay."

Before she could rebut his statement, he said, "Funny how that works, right? You think you've got everything going for you, but it was all just a big ol' fat lie and never existed in the first place."

"I'm sure if you talk with Liam, he'll let you stay above this place," she said, pointing to the ceiling. Liam had designed this place and had included a loft type space above this bar when it was built from the ground up after the fire took the old bar down—a not so great memory since it involved Leah's ex-boyfriend, but the outcome was good.

"Yeah, I might."

"Okay."

"Okay." She watched and waited for his next move. She wanted nothing more than to make him realize he had everything here in Cedar Valley, but mostly, she wanted him to realize he still had her. That she loved him with every fiber of her being. But for now, he was pushing away and she understood his frustration. Things were falling apart for him, but what he didn't realize was the fact he was in complete control of the outcome around here. He was the deciding factor in this whole mess he got himself into. "Promise me you won't leave town?"

She nearly choked on the words as she fought the tears threatening to escape. She needed to be badass, and she couldn't be badass if she had tears running down her cheeks, streaking her makeup.

"I can't make any promises, Meg," he said, chasing back yet another shot. If she had drunk the amount of alcohol he had in the last hour or so of their conversation, she would be lying on the floor in the fetal position crying. "I'm taking it one day at a time, but the outlook doesn't look too promising either."

The thought of him leaving again yanked at her heart, raced her thoughts in a tumbled mess, and made her want to tell him everything she felt about him just to prove there was something here for him.

The harder he shoved away from here, the closer she wanted to be with him. She refused to let him out of her life again.

10

Taking time away from the station was the perfect opportunity to hang out with his grandfather. Wes and Gramps would need help on the farm, especially if they were preparing cattle for the long haul with that Richards guy the women at the bar told him about.

The sun shined bright as it rested high above the mountain-lined sky. Not a cloud in sight. According to his watch, it was pushing the hour hand just past one. If he had to guess, Wes and his gramps would be just pulling in from their lunch at Granny Mae's Café, and they'd be antsy to get back out to the pasture.

Guiding the truck around the S curve, his grandfather's house came into view. Sitting atop its own hill, the two-story cabin welcomed visitors two miles down the road either way. The cabin had been built by Conner's great-grandfather and grandfather—back when his grandfather had been younger and stronger. He had aged well since then, but Conner knew the man was aging regardless and the time they had together shouldn't be taken for granted. He had learned that a few years ago when they lost his grandma on his mother's side. Grams was the one who settled family conflicts and kept the family together. She was the glue needed in the family, and the day she passed away was the day all hell broke loose and conflicts resurfaced.

Pulling his truck into the driveway, he drove over the ruts and through the potholes up to the house. Sure enough, Gramps and Wes were climbing out of the truck and grabbing their leftover containers from the café. Gramps took the container Wes was holding and walked toward the house.

Wes turned, sheltering the sun from his eyes, and waved at Conner. Conner nodded before shifting the truck into park. Grabbing his gloves and hat from the bench seat next to him, he opened the door and climbed out. With sunglasses on, he slipped his hat on top of his head and walked toward the two men pushing their mid-seventies.

"What brings you out here, son?" Wes asked, leaning against the bed of the truck. Gramps walked back from the house and waved at Conner. His gramps was happy to see him. It'd been a while since they'd had a visit with each other.

"I heard you're selling some cattle," Conner said, leaving out the part of how he knew. "Figured I'd come out here and see if you're needing help rounding them up."

Wes smiled, turned to Edward, and said, "Well, it wouldn't hurt to have an extra hand or two today."

Gramps looked over and nodded, agreeing without saying a word, and Conner knew he had come at the right time. These two men were the hardest workers he had ever seen, but that didn't mean he thought it was a good idea. The thought of the mid-day sun wiping them out, dehydrating them, was the concern Conner had with today's task at hand.

"All right," Conner said, clapping his hands together. "How many of these heifers are leaving?"

"They've got about a dozen heading out west over the next few days," Wes said, pointing to the cattle sectioned off to the south of where they were standing. "We've got them sorted and ready. Now we just need to grab Richards' trailer and load 'em up when he gets here."

"Sounds good," Conner said, taking a look around, noticing the trailer mentioned was nowhere to be found. "So, where's his trailer?"

"That's what we're wondering too," Gramps said, laughing. "He told us it'd be here after lunch today. We don't see it either."

Conner shook his head. What was the point of setting a time to load cattle if you wouldn't be here on time? He didn't have patience for waiting. "You get his number? Maybe we should call him and get an update?"

Wes shrugged and turned back toward the house. "I'll go ahead and give him a call. Maybe something came up." Wes pulled his phone out of the front pocket of his Tt-shirt and pressed some numbers. "Hey, it's Wes. We're out here at Ed's and wondering where your trailer is."

Wes' face scrunched as he listened to the person on the other end of the line. Conner hoped the guy was showing up here soon so they could get these cattle loaded sooner rather than later.

"Yeah, that'd be all right," Wes said, swiping a hand across his brow, the heat already taking a toll on him. "I've got Ed's grandson here to help out."

Wes glanced at Conner and looked back at Gramps before tossing an arm up in a *I've got no idea what the hell's going on* gesture. "All right, we'll keep our eye out for them. Sounds good, thanks."

Wes ended the call and shoved his phone back in his pocket. He walked back toward the truck and hollered, "Well, it seems Richards had something come up, left his nieces in charge of the trailer and they got lost."

The questionable statement coming out of Wes' mouth was exactly the thought Conner had. How the hell does someone get lost in Cedar Valley? A small town with only a few dirt roads. All they had to do was pull out on the highway and choose a damn road with the damn sign matching their address.

Walking back to the truck with Wes and Gramps, he caught wind of frustration coming from the men. They had plenty of other things needing done today and now they were running behind because of two girls who didn't know their heads from their asses.

"As soon as they get here, I'll help round the cattle and they'll be on their way in no time," Conner said, patting his Gramps on the back. "No worries."

"We've got a poker game tonight," Gramps said, making his way to the front porch. "I was hoping to have these cattle loaded and outta here right after lunch so I could get my nap in."

A muffled chuckle sounded in his throat. "You know I need my beauty sleep. You don't end up looking this good at this age by not sleeping."

"There's plenty of time for sleeping when you're dead, Ed," Wes said, laughing along with Conner. "And whoever's been telling you that you look good has bad eyes and needs glasses."

"I'll have you know they have perfect vision," Gramps said, jabbing an elbow into Conner with a shit-eating grin on his face. Conner had no idea who Gramps was referring to, but whoever it was, he was in agreeance with Wes.

Laughing, he shook his head. "What time's the game tonight? And where are they having it?"

"You're looking at the place," Gramps said, hitching a thumb over his shoulder in the direction of the cabin. "We've got the table set up all ready to go and everything. Your grandma wasn't too happy about it, but she'll just head over to Rosie's for coffee or something later."

Gramps looked at him. "Why? You needing something to do tonight? You don't have any plans?"

"Nope, can't say that I do," Conner admitted, knowing it seemed odd for a man in his twenties not to have plans on a Friday night. Well, he always had a backup plan to head to the bar if something else fell through, but it was a better idea to keep himself out of sight and out of mind for the night. He had to go into Levy's tomorrow night anyway. Liam had invited him to a dart tourney and he wasn't going to pass on the offer. He enjoyed throwing darts and anytime there was money involved was a good time to join in on the fun. "Besides, I can never turn down a good card game with the men."

"All right then, it starts at eight," Gramps said, patting Conner on the back. "Atta boy."

The crunching of gravel stirred their attention behind them. A Dodge truck, pulling an oversized trailer with two girls in the cab, headed up the driveway. The truck hit every pothole Conner had before coming to a complete stop and parking the truck as close to the men as they could.

The blonde opened the driver's side door and climbed out. "We're here."

"Finally," the brunette said, walking around the front of

the truck from the passenger side. "What's the saying about blondes and driving?"

The blonde glared at her from across the way before they walked toward the men. "It wasn't that bad." The blonde laughed, keeping her eyes on Conner. "You make it sound like we got lost a few times or about died."

"Maybe because we did get lost," the brunette said, rolling her eyes.

"You girls here for the cattle, I take it?" Wes asked, holding back his laughter. Conner couldn't help notice how ridiculous this situation was. For whatever reason their uncle had left them in charge of this operation, he hoped it was a good one. "You girls going to be able to handle that truck with a trailer full of cattle?"

The blonde shrugged her shoulders, still keeping her eyes focused on Conner. "I'm sure we can handle it from here."

Conner begged to differ, but what the hell did he know. Women were able to do anything they set their minds to, so he bit his tongue and enjoyed the view of two women not knowing what the hell they were in for.

LOADING THE CATTLE INTO THE TRAILER TOOK SOME time, but when it was done, it was done. He was thankful it hadn't taken longer. After making sure the women would be all right, and watching them drive down the road, Conner followed his gramps into the house.

Wes had ventured on home to clean up and prep for the night's poker game. It was just his gramps and him in the house now because his grandma had moseyed over to the

Spencers' house in order to leave the house for the guys tonight.

The smell of roast filled the air when he walked through the back door into the kitchen. He scrubbed his hands clean and dried them off before pulling out a couple of plates for him and his grandfather. His grandma was one helluva cook and never hesitated to leave food for them when she knew they would be hungry and in need.

"Gramps, how much are you wanting?" Conner called out to the living room where his grandfather was taking off his shoes. "I'll grab you some and meet you at the table."

"I've worked up quite the appetite. Go ahead and give me a plateful," Gramps said, making his way toward the dining room.

Conner scooped out enough potatoes and carrots, along with a few pieces of meat, onto the plates. There was no doubt in his mind they would get plenty to eat tonight.

Carrying the plates to the table, he set one in front of Gramps. "We'll have to thank Grams for this later."

Gramps winked and Conner thought about the love the two of them had shared all these years. They were coming up on their fiftieth anniversary and it didn't seem real how much love they had. Conner wanted something similar one day, but not yet. He was too focused on his career, or what was left of it anyway, to get caught up in a serious relationship with anyone who might not understand his tendencies to give one hundred percent to the job.

"What are you thinking about over there?" Gramps asked, dashing pepper on top of his food before taking another bite.

Conner could count on his Gramps for talking with him. There was never a time when Gramps hadn't been there for him. When he was a little kid, he would run to his

Gramps nine times out of ten to fix things for him. Nothing had changed over the last twenty years. He still came to his Gramps for help every now and then. He couldn't bear to think about a world without the man in it, but for right now, he was here and Conner was damned thankful for that.

"Your fiftieth anniversary is coming up," Conner said before shoving another bite into his mouth. Rounding cattle had taken damned near everything he had for energy and then some. Refueling was exactly what he needed.

"What's that gotta do with the price of tea in China?" Gramps cracked a smile followed by a slight chuckle.

"It's just got me thinking, is all," Conner said, taking time to gauge his grandfather's reaction, knowing his gramps was onto something already based on his facial expression.

"Thinkin' it's time to settle down, are ya?" Gramps asked, placing his used napkin on his plate before pushing back his chair. Conner watched him walk to the kitchen and place it in the sink after scraping it into the trash can. "Because if that's the case, I think I'll have to agree with ya."

Conner knew it was expected. It had been everyone's goal in this life to settle down, get married, and have kids, but for some reason, that goal hadn't been his and looking back, he had no regrets.

"What's got you thinking about love anyway?" Gramps asked, making his way back to the table. He shoved his chair back in under the table and turned back to face Conner. Motioning to the living room, he asked, "Wanna take this in there?"

Conner nodded, finishing off the last bite of food before taking his plate to the kitchen. He wasn't ready to talk about love and all of that mushy stuff with Gramps. He wasn't in the mood to discuss his nonexistent love life. His life was dull and boring when it came to that topic. Sure, he wanted a wife and a few kids someday, but right now, he had too much going on. With things going wrong, it wasn't the right time for anything but focus and determination.

Conner followed Gramps into the living room and chose the closest chair to sit in. Gramps sat in the recliner across the way.

"Tell me about what happened the other day on that fire call."

He didn't want to talk about that either. What had happened had been for the sake of the kid's life. He had acted on his instinct and what he had felt was right. He didn't regret a single minute of it. Consequences were just that, and sooner or later, things would go back to normal. But for now, things were messed up. "Things got overheated and blown way out of proportion."

"I've heard," Gramps said, nodding his head in agreeance.

Conner knew this small town would talk. The gossip around this place spread like wildfire. It spread faster than the fires in Colorado he had faced every day for the last two years.

"You want to talk about it?"

Conner shrugged and decided it wouldn't hurt. Gramps was the last person in this life who would judge a person, so it felt right to want to talk it over with him. Gramps was Switzerland when it came to firefighting and this family. Neutral and supportive.

"I heard the kid screaming and my instincts kicked in. That's all there was to it."

Nodding along, Gramps listened intently. He knew Gramps was understanding where Conner was coming from. Anyone with a heart would understand.

"Adam told me to stand down and I ignored him," he explained. "I didn't want to stand outside the fire and watch it burn while a kid was stuck inside. He shouldn't have wanted to either."

"Well, to be fair, he was just looking out for his crew, wasn't he?" Gramps asked, taking a sip from his glass that had been on the stand when they had entered the room. "In all honestly, I think both of you were right in your own ways. And I also think that's why neither of you can see the other's point."

Conner had to agree with Gramps. It was hard to be proved wrong, but it was harder to agree the other was right when what happened felt justified. "So now my job is on the line and I've got nowhere else to go. Adam's got the final say on my career and it's bugging the hell out of me. I can't imagine what I'm going to do if he kicks me off the service."

Gramps shook his head and took another drink from his glass. "I don't think you have anything to worry about. Adam knows what he's working with and he knows you're young," he said. "And I can almost bet my life's savings on the fact he's waiting for your next move."

Conner's brow raised and Gramps said, "The ball's in your court. You have the next move. You have complete control over the outcome of your own destiny. What you choose to say or do from here on out makes the difference between having something or losing it."

Gramps had a point. He had a lot to lose and where he would like to pass blame on Adam and make him out to be the bad guy, Conner knew that was not how it worked. It wasn't how any of this worked. He needed to own up to his mistakes and overcome the consequences. Regardless if Adam believed in him or not was mute compared to the determination and confidence Conner had in himself.

"That goes for your love life too," Gramps said. "Because I know you're thinking about your future and I also know you're wanting what everyone else has. Spending a hundred percent of your time and energy on a job isn't going to give anything but money. And you know what they say about money and happiness. It's something money can't buy."

"You've got a point," Conner said, making his way to the kitchen. A drink was calling his name. It was half past seven and the card game would start soon enough.

"Or two," Gramps called out behind him. "I've been there, done that, and was lucky enough to realize it when I was still young. That's how I found your grandmother. She caught me and never let me go."

Cracking open a can of beer, Conner tipped back and emptied the contents within a minute. Thirst had a lot to do with it, but thoughts needed drowned out and lately the only thing that worked to silence them was booze—and a lot of it.

"When's everyone going to be here?" he asked, pulling out a chair at the card table. The table was set up with cards, poker chips, and in the center of it all was a box of cigars and snacks. The perfect combination for a great night. "I'm ready to win some money."

Gramps made his way over to the table and chose the same chair he had for the last five years of playing cards. He had the head of the table and the view of the whole show.

"They'll be here before you know it," Gramps said, shuffling the deck. A smile crept onto his face. "I've heard Megan might be coming too. That'll raise the stakes a bit more, won't it?"

His Gramps had no idea how true that statement was. The thought of her showing up made his heart race.

Thoughts of her had overwhelmed him over the last few days. Things had changed between them, but he loved her. It was confusing, and he wasn't sure if he was going to tell her how he truly felt or not. Hell, as far as he knew, it could be Stockholm syndrome from her rescuing him in the midst of hell.

11

Walking into Granny Mae's Café, Megan clung to the nagging feeling to check on Conner. She hadn't seen or heard from him in the last week, since the whole situation with the house fire. She had gone through great lengths to save him from that house, and not to mention from Adam's wrath hovering over disciplinary actions.

"Meg, I'm so glad you're here," Granny Mae called out to her, offering a friendly smile with an over enthusiastic wave. She loved Granny Mae and was thankful she and her grandmother had started this business adventure together. "Rosie's been waiting all morning for you to get here."

Granny Mae waved off the inclination that sentence created and said, "But I'm sure it's just the whole grandmother thing again."

The sweet woman winked and offered a freshly baked muffin to Megan across the counter. "This is for you...on the house," Granny Mae whispered with the sweetest grandmotherly smile on her face.

"Aww, thank you," Megan said, accepting the treat even

though her stomach was a bundle of nerves. Over the last few days, her thoughts had trailed near and far over the possibility of losing Conner once again. On top of that fear, she had been ignoring calls from her grandmother and she knew today would be a heated discussion between them. But, she was here, and she would rather have that conversation face-to-face than over the phone.

"I'll let her know you're here, honey," Granny Mae patted Megan's hand and walked away from the counter toward the back room.

The muffin tasted pretty good—as far as the pieces she picked apart. Her nerves were getting the best of her. A part of her wanted to leave and not look back, another part wanted to admit to her grandmother that she had been right —she wasn't cut out for this fire stuff. But shoving it all aside, she knew she wanted nothing more than to do what she'd been doing. She had the best of both worlds.

"Oh, Meg," her grandmother's words cut through the thoughts tumbling around in her head. "I'm so glad you're okay."

Putting the muffin down on the plate, Megan turned in her seat and opened her arms for her grandmother's embrace. Rosie placed a quick kiss on her cheek while holding on tight to Megan. Deep down, the risk of losing the battle against fires scared the crap out of her, but she wouldn't let others see that fear. Her grandmother, on the other hand, could sense it and Megan's doubts fueled Rosie's attempt to talk Megan out of fighting fires.

"I'm fine, Grandma," Megan whispered, patting her grandmother's back as they swayed by the counter. "I'm fine."

Wet cheeks touched hers as her grandmother pulled away from her to look into her eyes. "You had me so scared," she admitted, taking hold of Megan's hand and led her back to the table. "I heard the trucks go out, and people were saying how bad the fire was, and the first thought I had was to pray for you."

Some people would never be okay with the risks of this job, and Megan respected that. Some would never understand the meaning behind giving so much to this line of work, but Megan wouldn't give up trying to make them understand. There was more to this job than chasing fires. It was the feeling of doing good. Helping people on the worst day of their lives. Nothing compared to responding to fires and medical calls.

"And then I heard you ran in after that Conner boy and I about lost it," her grandmother's tone changed, from needing reassurance to demanding Megan to hear her out. Megan was listening and refused to interrupt her grandmother's concerns. Rosie had every right to feel the way she did, and Megan couldn't change the way she felt. "What would make you run in after him, Megan?"

When she wanted to shrug, she knew better. Her grandmother didn't like shrugging. She found it as a sign of disrespect and a lack of interest in what was being said. Instead, she looked into the eyes similar to her own and said, "I didn't have a choice, Grandma."

Rosie shook her head, and to their rescue, Granny Mae moseyed over to their table and set down a plate full of breakfast—scrambled eggs, bacon, and toast.

"Let's eat."

Megan was relieved by the quick save. She was hungry like no other and right now, she didn't have the answers her grandmother was wanting to hear. She loved Conner. She loved fighting fires. She especially loved saving people. The perfect combination to make her misstep and cross a line she should have never crossed. Ruining her career and her friendship was the last thing she ever wanted to do. Saving Conner was something she had to do, but falling in love with him...that was something she had no control over.

"There's something about saving those Jacobsen boys, isn't there?" Rosie said, cutting her toast in half. "You just can't help yourself when it comes to saving people."

Megan nodded with a mouth full of food. Her grandmother was right. "It's my job," she said, grabbing her glass of milk and taking a drink.

"No," Rosie said, shaking her head while chewing on her food. She pointed a warning finger at Megan while balancing the fork in front of her face. "It's not your job to save everyone. It's your job to listen to commands and follow through with them."

Megan remained quiet as she chewed her food. Keeping her eyes down at the table, she knew it was better not to say anything, even though her grandmother wanted her to. There was so much to say, but she would wait it out. Right now, her grandmother was frustrated and venting. When things calmed down a bit, Megan would explain.

Granny Mae interrupted the silence by complimenting the cook. A laugh erupted when they realized she was wanting recognition for a tasty breakfast. Megan leaned over and patted Granny's hand. "Thank you for making us breakfast, Gran. It tastes really good and it's hitting the spot."

Granny smiled and looked at Rosie, waiting for her to acknowledge breakfast, but Rosie kept her focus on her plate and said, "Thanks."

Granny looked back at Megan with a shocked look. Megan nodded and mouthed the words "she's mad at me" and frowned. In return, Granny patted her hand and whispered she knew exactly why Megan did what she did. Megan smiled and mouthed a thank you before watching Granny Mae stand and clear the table, leaving Rosie and Megan alone once again.

"Megan, I love you," Rosie said, locking her eyes on her. "I understand you're chasing dreams and all, but you're risking your life. The last thing I want is to lose my granddaughter because she was selfless and not thinking about herself."

Odd request, but Megan understood. The last thing people wanted was for you to be selfish, unless not being selfish would take you away from them.

"I knew what I was doing, I promise," Megan said, trying her hardest to get Rosie to understand. "Adam commanded to stand down, but watching Conner run into that house after hearing the kid's cry for help pulled me after him. I had to make sure he got out of there okay. He needed me to have his back. And I know he would have done the same thing if it had been the other way around."

Rosie nodded, this time remaining silent until she collected the right words. "You're right, he probably would. Any of them would have done the same exact thing, except they didn't and you did. You're lucky you both made it out of that house."

Megan knew the odds that day had been against her and she was more than thankful they had made it out of that house—together and with the child—that alone had made it all worth it. Every last minute was worth it when they had brought the kid out of the house.

"Chasing fires is one thing, but chasing your heart is another and if you're not careful, it'll get you hurt," Rosie warned, taking a sip of coffee. Megan looked at her like she had lost her mind mentioning it, but Rosie shook her head.

"I know why you did it. Well, I mean the other half of the reason you did it. You love him. I know."

Megan was speechless. She knew she and her grandmother were close, but she didn't think it was that obvious how she felt about Conner. Was he the only one oblivious to how she truly felt?

"You've loved him for a long time and now it's interfering with keeping yourself safe," Rosie said, making sure Megan was paying attention. "And that worries me. I remember when I was young like you and let my heart stand in the way of many things. My heart also led me astray a few too many times. I quickly learned to put aside emotions and act on logic and common sense first. The emotions can come later."

Megan nodded. The same thoughts her grandmother was sharing had crossed her mind from time to time. Keeping emotions out of the way meant keeping herself from danger.

"I guess what I'm saying is," Rosie continued, "you've got to keep yourself out of danger's way no matter how much you love that boy."

She heard what her grandmother was saying loud and clear. She thought Conner was trouble now. Everyone in town thought that. They all talked and talk was cheap in a small town. They all thought he was immature and reckless, risking it all to get the job done, including everyone's lives.

But they didn't know Conner like she did. He was the kindest, most sensitive man she'd ever known and he would do anything for anyone without hesitation. Sure, he was careless on a call or two, but anyone can make the same mistakes. She knew the real Conner and she would always have his back—no matter what her grandmother or anyone else had to say.

12

It had been a little over a week since his last shift. Adam had called him last night, confirming his shift for today. Conner knew better than to tell Adam to get lost. They had settled their differences over last night's phone conversation, and even though Conner still felt what he did was right, he had to respect Adam and his authority. Making amends meant promising to keep his head in the game and stay focused on what was expected of him.

Adam had asked him about coming back *home* as in staying at his and Rachel's house, but that had been a hard no. He told Adam too much wedding talk and mushy stuff was happening lately. He loved his brother and his future sister-in-law, but weddings were overrated and all the talk had been driving him bonkers over the last few months. Plus, it did him good to stay in the loft above the bar. Especially on nights he drank too much and he didn't have to worry about going too far or driving. Living above Levy's wasn't where he expected to end up, but it worked.

"Hey, long time no see," the newbie called out to him as

he pushed through the entrance into the lounge area. "Where've you been?"

It was nice to know the talk around here hadn't corrupted the newbie's impression of him. The last thing he wanted was for one more person to think he was a monster—even though he sometimes felt like one, it wasn't his intention.

"Hey, Noob," Conner said, walking over to the couch after grabbing the TV remote. "I took a mini vacation. It's good to take those every now and again, ya know?"

The newbie laughed and nodded. "It's been a while since I've been able to take one. I'm actually forgetting what they are."

Conner laughed. There's no telling how long it had been since he had taken an actual vacation. This last week was unintentional, but it worked out for the best for all involved that he checked himself out.

"So, where'd you go? Anywhere nice?" the newbie said, leaning forward, fully invested in anything Conner had to say.

"Depends on where you'd say is *nice*," Conner said, a subtle chuckle as he watched the newbie's expression as he pondered over the perfect destination.

"Colorado sounds nice," the newbie said, without realizing he mentioned a sore spot for Conner. "Or Minnesota."

"Minnesota? What's there to do in Minnesota?" Conner had never been to Minnesota, but he couldn't think of a single thing for tourists to do up that way.

Newbie shrugged, keeping his expression neutral. "I have some family up there and haven't seen them in a while."

"Ah, I see," Conner said, kicking himself in the ass for being a jerk. Made sense he would put his foot in his mouth yet again. One day he would think before saying something he might regret. Ha, that was easier said than done. It would take him forever to get the hang of that. "Why Colorado, Noob?"

"I love the mountains," the kid said, smiling from ear to ear. "I've always wanted to go there, but you know finding the time and money...never works out for me."

"I hear ya there," Conner said, leaning forward, resting his arms on his knees. "I just moved back from there. It's a beautiful place, but, man, I'll tell ya the fires aren't so friendly."

They got a laugh out of that, but Conner's mind flashed to the flames that had surrounded his friends, taking their lives in a flicker. *Damn.* Shaking his head, he tried to avoid that discussion. No new kid would want to hear the risks of this job—if they hadn't already figured it out for themselves.

"I've heard about those fires that claimed your friends' lives," the kid said, his facial expression remaining solemn as he continued, "I'm sorry things had to be so rough out there for you, man."

Conner shrugged. Tears welled in his eyes, but in order to keep the tough exterior impression, he had no choice but to shrug it off. "It happens."

Refusing to talk about it didn't do any good, but talking about it didn't either. Bringing more pain into the equation wouldn't promise him better days. The alcohol helped soothe his pain. That was as far as he was willing to go.

"I can't imagine," the kid said, keeping his eyes on Conner, expecting him to talk about something he had no idea how far down he had shoved those damn memories. If Conner had to guess, the kid's friends were all still alive, never having to face the ugly effects of losing a buddy or two. Not that Conner wished that hell on anyone, but knowing the kid was still young—younger than him—told him he was a few years short on experience. "I know you're probably thinking I wouldn't have a clue."

Conner looked over at the kid, ready for what the kid was about to say to prove his assumptions wrong.

"My dad lost his life," he said, wringing his hands together, the subject a tough one to talk about. "Not to chasing fires or anything hero like, but to cancer. To me, he was a hero, but to everyone else, not so much."

Conner sat speechless, watching the kid divulge the details of his father's diagnosis and the road to a dead end. A sucker punch to the gut and he still had no words for the kid. Damn. Here he had thought the kid hadn't experienced loss in this life. The saying of making an ass from assuming was the most truthful thing he'd ever heard as of right now.

"I'm sorry to hear that," Conner said, finally able to get a grip and find some words. Him and his father were at each other's throats nine times out of ten, but the thought of losing the old man paralyzed him in fear. The thought of losing either parent, or brother, had him wishing death wouldn't come knocking on doors.

"It was rough, but his final wish was for me to go out and make something of myself," the kid explained. "He and I had several talks up until the day he died. It wasn't like we weren't close, but the talks were awkward. I was in denial. I hated to admit I was losing my dad. But I had promised him I would chase after my dreams."

Conner sat quietly listening to the kid recall his conversations with his dad. The kid was emotional, and it tugged on Conner's heart to hear the damn stories, but he knew it did the kid good to get it out—to talk to someone about it. Something he needed to tell himself.

"So, here I am," the kid said, glancing around while

showcasing the lounge area with his arms. "Chasing fires and making something of myself like my dad requested."

Conner could see the regret written on the kid's face. He was no expert at this talking thing, or reading people's expressions, but something told him the kid was having doubts about choosing this path in his life. "Not what you were expecting, huh?"

The kid looked up at Conner, a deer in the headlights look, knowing he had said too much, or maybe not enough, but either way, the doubt had spilled out for all to see. Thankfully, it was just Conner here. He'd make it his job to help this kid through this. There was no way he'd allow this kid to give up and continue to regret whatever regret he would have for not following through with his promise to his dad.

"When I was your age," Conner said, laughing at the thought. "What, four years ago?"

The kid laughed. "Yeah, probably."

"I joined the service to make my dad proud, too," Conner said, recalling the memories from so long ago. The memories that had ended up getting shoved down deep with the others over time. "But the only difference between your story and mine, is my dad's still alive. But, and that's a big but," he warned while holding up a finger to pause the kid's reflection on the thought. "He's been dead to me for so long now that I'm not sure how to fix what went wrong. Hell, I don't even know what went wrong or why he's so unhappy with me."

"Why don't you just talk to him?"

"If only it were that easy, I would've by now," Conner admitted, an anger filled sadness twisted in his gut. "You see, my dad ain't easy to talk to. And this conflict between us, well, it's been ongoing since I was, oh hell, I don't know, ten? Eleven? Hell, I hadn't even known there was a problem until I graduated from high school. I always thought he was just a grumpy old man who was tired after raising my brother. Who, mind you, was the perfect son any father could ask for. I wasn't. I had made plenty of dumb choices. Hell, I still do."

"Why not just call him out on it?" The kid was fully invested in the outcome of this conversation. Conner could tell the kid had a good relationship with his father. Conner's wasn't easy—it never had been once he hit double digits.

"I've tried, but it turns into one big altercation and honestly, it isn't worth seeing my dad that angry just to settle the conflict. Things get pretty heated and it only makes things worse. The pain in my mother's face is almost too much to bear and it's almost like my father's too stubborn to realize how wrong he is for holding a grudge against me. A grudge for what? I have no idea. That I was born? Maybe. Hell, it'd be nice if he just came right out and told me, but I don't see that happening anytime soon."

"Dang," the kid said, shaking his head. "And here I thought my dad had been stubborn. I'm sorry it's been like that for ya."

Conner shrugged it off. "It's life. You can't always get your way and sometimes things aren't so clear."

Before the kid could get up and walk away from their conversation, Conner said, "Before you get going, hear me out for a minute. The kid sat back down and kept his eyes on Conner. "Before you give up, or think about quitting, look at how far you've come and remember this talk we've had today. Things get rough, it's not easy, no one said it was, but know there's a reason we're here. There's a reason we're on this service, and whether it's because of our dads or not, it's because we want to be. In the end, we want this as much as the next guy."

The kid stood, stretched, and extended a hand in Conner's direction. "Thanks, man."

Conner stood, taking hold of the kid's hand with a firm grip. "You bet, Noob," he said, patting the kid on the back with his free hand. "It's okay if I call you that, right?"

The kid shrugged. "Well, once I'm not so green, you can call me Chase."

"Chase chasin' fires," Conner teased. "I like it."

Laughing their way out to the truck bay, Conner reached into his pocket and pulled out his phone. He was going to take a few minutes and call his father. Whether or not it would end well, he was about to find out.

13

Climbing out of her car in Adam's driveway, she recognized Ava's laugh coming from the front porch before actually finding the little girl sitting on her mother's lap. Rachel was best friends with Leah, but they had invited Megan into their circle soon after Leah's car accident. At first, Megan had felt like an intruder, a third wheel in the friendship, but that soon changed and the three of them were known around town as the *Three Amigos*. Not so original, but it worked.

"Hey, Meg," Rachel called out to her as Megan entered the front yard and made her way to the porch steps. "We were just talking about how much fun you guys are going to have tonight while Mommy and Daddy go out."

Megan had offered to watch the kids tonight so Adam and Rachel could have a night out together. With two kids, Megan knew the chances of their alone time had to slim to none. The least she could do would be to watch the kids overnight so the parents could enjoy themselves.

"Yes, of course," Megan said, clapping her hands before reaching out to Ava, who gladly accepted the invite into her arms. "I've got so much planned for the night. We're going to play outside, order pizza, and watch movies."

"Pizza!" Ava cheered, clapping her hands wildly as Megan cheered right along with her, spinning them around in a circle.

"Auntie Megan knows what little Miss Ava would like," she said, setting her down on the porch floor before pulling out a small bag of animal crackers from her overnight bag. "Look what I brought."

Ava's smile beamed brightly, showing her gap-toothed smile that Megan adored. There was something about a toddler and their cheeky grins with missing teeth that left Megan wanting her own children someday. That someday wouldn't come too soon, so for right now, she would love on Rachel and Adam's kiddos and be the best *auntie* she could possibly be.

Ripping open the baggie of crackers, she squatted down and handed a couple to Ava, who was more than ready to get her mouth on them. "Auntie also brought another surprise for you and Tyler."

Rachel raised an eyebrow and chuckled. Megan knew what she was thinking, and she was exactly right. These kids were spoiled by her and she had no regrets. She didn't have nieces or nephews of her own. Her sister had refused to have kids as she ventured off into the business world. Shaking away the thoughts of how much she missed her sister and how much their conversations had suffered because of the distance between them, Megan turned back to Rachel and offered her an animal cracker with a smile on her face. "You know I love these kiddos like they're my own," she said, offering another cracker to Ava, who had eaten two crackers faster than Megan thought possible. "Besides, auntie's my name and spoiling kids is my game."

Winking, Megan danced around the porch with Ava watching her with big round eyes. That little girl would grow up to be a heartbreaker, and the only one to blame for that would be her mama for giving her those looks. "Just think, soon enough, they're going to be older and not wanting us to dote on them."

Rachel frowned at the thought of her babies growing up.

Megan pointed at her and said, "That's exactly why I can't refuse to spoil these kiddos."

"Okay, okay, don't make me cry," Rachel said, fanning her eyes, laughing at Ava, who was now boogying in a circle just like Megan had done a few minutes ago. "You're going to mess up my makeup."

Megan shook her head and swept Ava off her feet. Now that her mouth was empty, Megan was able to spin her around and make her laugh. "Tell Mommy she better get going if she's gonna, otherwise she'll be late for her date with Daddy."

Rachel stood from the porch swing and wrapped her arms around Megan and Ava both, planting a kiss on the side of Ava's head. "Okay, I'll get going, but promise me you won't have too much fun."

Megan wrapped her free arm around Rachel, pulling her in for one last hug. "I make no promises, but I'm sure we'll have a blast. Enjoy your night out with your soon-to-be hubby."

Rachel tossed her head back laughing, then tucked a loose hair behind her ear before heading inside to grab her purse and tell Tyler goodbye. Megan could hear Tyler racing toward the front door just as she opened it and caught him in her free arm. Ava laughed and reached out for Tyler, who, like any good big brother, gladly accepted her and carried her back inside. Megan followed close behind, giving Rachel one last hug before she strolled out the door.

"If you need anything, don't hesitate to call," Rachel said, turning back before walking out the door. Megan nodded, knowing they wouldn't have to call anyone except the pizza place for supper. "Have fun, kids. And be good." One final hug and kiss to each of the kids and Rachel was out the door. The kids didn't watch her get in the car and leave. Instead, they hurried to Megan's side and begged for her to play games.

"Of course! But first, what do you say we order pizza?"

"Yeah!" Both kids hollered in unison as they hopped in place. It was hard to believe Tyler was nearing teenage years, because he was still so young at heart. She loved his demeanor and positive attitude. No parent could ask for a happier kid than Tyler. "What kind? Can we order pepperoni?" Tyler asked, hands together as he prayed she'd say yes.

"Is that the kind you both want?" she asked, looking at Ava, who nodded her head in agreeance with her brother. "Okay, then let's get it ordered so we can play outside."

Megan grabbed her phone and hit speed dial for the pizza place. Taking less than five minutes, the pizza was ordered and had an arrival time of thirty to forty minutes.

Ushering the kids outside, she asked what games they would like to play while they still had time before dark. Both kids suggested two randomly different options, with their age difference being the main reason behind it. Tyler, of course, mentioned football, and it hadn't surprised her one bit. That kid played football all hours of the day, and when he wasn't playing football or in school, he was baking with Rachel. Ava, on the other hand, loved playing *chalk*. Megan enjoyed doodling on the back patio with her, drawing everything from turtles to balloons, to puppies and elephants. She had never been the best artist, but Ava sure enjoyed watching her draw and that was all that mattered.

"Okay, how about we play catch with Tyler for a little bit, and then we can color with chalk?" Megan suggested, knowing Ava would more than likely agree with her and go along with anything as long as it was fun.

Within minutes, they were worn out from playing football with Tyler and drawing with chalk on the concrete patio. Ava encouraged Megan to draw a clown with animal balloons, which meant she had recently gone to the town circus and had a new obsession. The last time Megan drew with her, it had been puppies and kitties, because the town veterinarian had brought them to the daycare.

"Do you want a boy or girl clown?"

"Girl!" Ava shrieked, her arms raised way above her head. "With a big nose!"

"Okay, a big nose and big shoes too?"

"Yeah," Ava said, sitting down beside Megan as she watched her draw the making of the clown.

"Is she a happy clown or a sad clown?" Megan asked, making facial expressions for each emotion.

"Happy!"

"Okay, what's her name going to be?" Megan asked, quickly drawing the clown to match Ava's requests. A glance at her watch told her the food would be here any minute and they still needed to wash up.

"Dolly!" Ava said, excited with the finishing touches Megan added to the clown's outfit.

"Dolly it is," Megan said, drawing a name tag on a balloon floating near the clown before filling it in with the name Dolly. "All done. Do you like it?"

Ava clapped her hands and smiled. "Yay!"

Megan looked over at what Tyler had drawn and was surprised to see the boy had some mad art skills as he finished up his masterpiece. "Is there anything you're not good at?" Megan asked, teasing him with a nudge. "You're making Aunt Meg look like a wannabe compared to you, Mr. Picasso."

Hiding a shy smile, Tyler colored in the last of his football player. "I've always liked to draw."

"Well, I can see why," Megan said, tousling the boy's hair. "What do you say we head inside and get washed up? The food should be here any minute now."

The kids raced each other inside, little Ava barely able to catch up to her brother, but he held the door open for her, offering her a high five on her way by. If Megan had a choice in the matter, she would love her kids to be like Tyler and Ava. They were the sweetest kids anyone would meet and Megan longed for sweet kids like them someday.

Herding the kids to the kitchen, making sure they scrubbed their dirty hands, she tossed them a towel right before the doorbell rang. "I'll be right back," she said, holding up a finger before leaving the kitchen. "Tyler, if you want to grab plates and set the table, that'd be awesome!" She hollered over her shoulder on her way to the door.

"One large pepperoni pizza?" the boy asked, confirming her order. "That'll be ten sixteen."

Handing him a twenty, she told him to keep the change before taking the pizza and carrying it into the dining room. Tyler had done as she asked, which was super, so she set the pizza down in the center of the table and served them a couple slices each. She reached for Ava's fork and cut up her slices into smaller, square bites.

She thought about what they would do after supper,

knowing Ava would possibly clonk out soon after her bath. Being a toddler was hard work and tiring.

"What kind of movies do you guys like to watch?" Megan asked, watching Ava's eyes widen in excitement.

"*Frozen*!" She had a mouthful of food, but that didn't stop her from suggesting her all-time favorite movie.

"You still like *Frozen*?" Megan asked, knowing the movie was more than a couple years old.

"She watches it nonstop," Tyler said, taking another bite of his pizza. "Sometimes, I like to think the movie player will burn up just so we don't have to watch it a million times a day."

Megan laughed while Ava pouted, her bottom lip jutting out. "That's not nice."

Tyler rolled his eyes and stabbed another piece of pizza. "What's not nice is making us watch it over and over again. I know the movie by heart. Would you like me to act it out for you?"

Ava clapped, laughing at her brother's hysterical dramatics. Tyler may have been upset about watching *Frozen* over and over again, but he was having fun acting out a scene from the movie.

"Okay, well, since Tyler did such an awesome job acting out a couple scenes from the movie, how about we let him pick what we watch tonight?" Megan asked, crossing her fingers while hoping this didn't send Ava into a hysterical frenzy of uncontrollable fits.

Jutting her bottom lip out, Ava looked down with crocodile tears welling up. Just when Megan thought the crying would start, Ava nodded and smiled.

"Whew, that went better than I thought it would," Megan said to Tyler on their way into the living room. "What movie are we going to watch?"

"*Transformers*!" Tyler said, making his way to the movie cabinet along the wall. "Have you seen them?"

Megan thought about the movies she had watched in the last year or so. A lot of Hallmark romance and romcoms, but she couldn't recall watching the Transformers. "Nope, I don't think I have."

"You're going to love them! Just wait and see!" Tyler said, reaching into the cabinet and bringing the movie for her to put into the DVD player. "I love Bumblebee!"

"Is he an actual bee?" Megan asked, wondering where else a name like that would come from.

"Nooo silly," Tyler said, plopping down on his section of the couch. "They're robots that turn into cars and trucks! Semis too!"

Megan slowly nodded. "That makes sense. So why Bumblebee?"

Tyler shrugged and pressed play on the remote control. "You'll just have to watch and see for yourself. I think he's the best!"

Ava crawled into Megan's lap as soon as the movie started. She would almost bet the little one would be fast asleep before a quarter of the way into the movie.

Pulling a blanket off the back of the couch, she cuddled with Ava as they watched the movie. Action-packed and entertaining was an understatement. Megan wondered why she had never seen this movie before.

Hours passed, the movie ended, and the kids were passed out. Ava had snuggled fast asleep against her, making it hard for Megan to want to move her. She enjoyed holding a sleeping babe in her arms, but she needed to get the mess from dinner cleaned up and the movie put away.

Carrying Ava upstairs to her toddler bed, Megan quietly adjusted the musical nightlight on the stand and made sure it would play softly while little Ava dreamed of clowns and circus animals.

Kissing Ava's head, she whispered good night and slowly made her way out of the room as she left the door cracked open a tiny fraction of an inch just in case.

Making her way back downstairs, she was surprised to see Tyler rounding up his blankets and making his way toward her. "Ready for bed, bud?"

Rubbing sleepy eyes, he nodded as she turned to walk with him upstairs. Opening his door, she followed him into his room and pulled back the covers. He hopped into bed and offered her a hug she couldn't refuse. "Thank you, Aunt Meg."

"You're welcome, buddy," she whispered, running a hand through his thick hair. "I hope you had fun tonight."

"Which transformer is your favorite?" he asked, his tired eyes trying hard to stay open long enough for her to answer his question.

"I would have to agree with you on this one," she said, smiling down at him. "Bumblebee won my heart. He's definitely my favorite and one of the best."

She winked and gave him one final hug before tucking him in tight. Walking toward the door, she could hear his soft snores. Like with Ava's door, she left his open a smidge just in case and ventured back downstairs.

IT WAS NEARING TEN O'CLOCK AND EVEN THOUGH SHE should have been dog tired, she wasn't. She was watching a Hallmark movie and the night was still young. Watching mushy movies was her thing, but sometimes she felt a pang of envy while watching them. She sometimes wished for a simple life that included the love of her life and a happy ever after.

She hadn't believed in happily ever after since fairy tales, but it would be nice if they did exist, for her to receive hers. She and Rosie would watch Hallmark for hours on end, and Wes would tease about the mushiness they were watching. He would sometimes mention how cliché the movies were, but she and Rosie would beg to differ. It didn't matter what a man thought about Hallmark movies, women all over the world continued to find hope while watching them.

A clink at the door, followed by a subtle unlock of the dead bolt caught her by surprise as she stood to combat the intruder. She knew Rachel would have at least texted her to let her know they were on their way home, if in fact they were. The thought of Adam coming home to grab something they may have forgotten crossed her mind but was quickly dismissed when the intruder opened the door and met her face-to-face.

"Conner?"

"Megan?" he said, an expression full of concern written on his face. "What are you doing here?"

She crossed her arms over her braless frame. "I could ask you the same thing."

Rubbing a hand over the back of his neck, he looked down at the floor and back up at her. "Sorry, I didn't mean for it to come out like that."

"Okay, but why are you here?" she asked, insistent on knowing the reason behind the late night visit. "I thought you were staying above Levy's now?"

"I was," he said, "I mean, I am."

Raising an eyebrow, she wondered what the heck he

was up to tonight. Apparently, he had a few too many drinks and found himself lost at his brother's house.

"I just thought I would come talk to my brother, but I take it he's not here?"

"They went out tonight. They'll be back tomorrow."

Short, sweet, and to the point. She hated that he was drunk and showing up here at this hour. The last thing she wanted was for him to wake the kids, especially this late at night.

Surprised to see him still standing there inside the door, she waited for him to say something to clear the awkwardness between them.

As if on cue, he pointed to the television and said, "You're watching this cheesy movie?"

"It's not cheesy," she said, furrowing her brows at him. Besides, what did he know about cheesy movies?

"If you say so," he said, chuckling as he walked over to the couch to sit down. "Let me guess. She bumped into him at the local diner and hasn't seen him in years. They were the best of friends, tried love once but failed, and now they're rekindling the old flame?"

"Wow, sounds like you've watched a few too many of these movies." Megan couldn't help but notice a guilty grin tug at his lips. "Thought so."

"What can I say? I'm a hopeless romantic."

Throwing her head back, laughing hysterically at his witty reply, she couldn't help but fall more in love with him.

14

Coming to Adam's may have been a mistake, but since he was there, and Megan too, he decided to make the most of the situation. He had a lot of making up to do when it came to Megan and he may as well start tonight.

He hadn't treated her so great the last few times he'd been around her, but he was determined to make things right. He couldn't control his mood, or the fact he had taken up drinking to soothe his pain, but he could control his attitude toward her. She had done nothing to deserve his asshole ways, and the fact that he deeply cared for her made it possible for him to change.

"Okay, listen," he said, pulling her attention from the cheesy Hallmark movie she'd been watching before his arrival. "You gotta promise me you won't laugh."

Her raised eyebrow told him she was waiting to hear something good, but not promising she wouldn't laugh.

"Pinky promise?" he asked, holding out his finger for her to do her part. "Come on, or I won't tell you."

"What's in it for me?" she asked hesitantly before meeting him in the middle with her outstretched pinky. "I mean, I already know you watch these shows in your downtime. What more is there to know? What else could you say that would surprise me?"

Laughing, he hooked her pinky with his and said, "You just wait."

She yanked her finger back and held it like he had cooties and they were in sixth grade again. Back when things were simple and their friendship had prospered past the unimportant arguments over who was on whose team for dodgeball.

"That's not fair," she whined, her bottom lip jutting out as she gave him sad eyes. "I didn't want to promise. What if I laugh?"

She was adorable sitting next to him on the couch. He wanted nothing more than to be able to lean over and kiss those pouting lips of hers. Kiss her and show her that clichés do exist and cheesy Hallmark movies were only the beginning of something far better in this life.

"It's okay if you laugh," he said, offering her his cheesy grin. "I would probably laugh too if it were me in your spot."

"Okay."

"Okay." He inhaled a deep breath and let it out slowly. There were several things she didn't know about him, but after what he was about to tell her, he would no longer be able to act rough and tough around her. His man card might be stolen for what he was about to admit. He didn't care, but then again, he kind of did. Only because they had known each other for so long did he feel comfortable with sharing his deepest, darkest mushiness.

"I used to watch Hallmark all the time when we were in high school," he said, holding his breath while waiting for her reaction. Only when she had no reaction, he said, "That's it. That's my secret."

"Okay, I already knew that," she said, not surprised by his confession one bit.

"How? How'd you already know?"

Laughing now, she crossed her legs in front of her and turned to face him. "Do you not remember a few minutes ago when you admitted you're a hopeless romantic?"

"Ah, I forgot about that," he said, rubbing a hand at the base of his neck. It was hard to believe he had said that, let alone forget he had said it. He blamed it on the alcohol. He had too many shots and way too many beers with the guys at Levy's tonight. He had only drunk so much in order to get enough courage to come talk to his brother. Now, it was wasted courage because his brother wasn't here. He and his future wife were probably making love and discussing their future while hidden away from the world in a hotel room. A pang of envy tore his attention back to Megan.

"Sorry, I had a few too many before coming here tonight," he admitted, smiling at her, hoping she didn't think he was a drunk idiotic loser. Most likely, she did, but she wouldn't say so, because she was polite like that, sweet like that. "I just needed an extra bout of courage in order to say the things I needed to say to Adam."

"I understand," she said, a smile tugging at those kissable lips of hers. Damn how much he wanted to come clean and risk it all just to tell her how much he loved her, but she would most likely blame it on the alcohol and tell him he'd lost his mind. "Adam just wants the best for you. You know that, right?"

Instead of risking a friend, he decided to keep his mouth shut about his feelings and just have a normal conversation with her, like old times. The old times like before he left Cedar Valley for Colorado.

"Yeah, I get it," he said, ignoring the urge to run for a

beer in the fridge. She probably wouldn't mind, but the last thing he wanted was for anyone to think he had a drinking problem. "But I still think he overreacted about the house fire. You and I both know I did nothing wrong."

He watched her pained expression as she hesitated her words. "I see both sides, actually. You almost got yourself killed. Which is what Adam was not wanting to happen," she said, keeping her voice low, barely above a whisper. "But you saved that boy and proved you could handle any situation thrown your way. Or at least until you couldn't."

Another pained expression crossed her face. A look of fear at the thought that had likely came to her mind. "You almost died."

"I know," he said, knowing full well there was no way he could deny the facts. The truth was brutal when it came time to face it. What he did was selfless, of course, but what if he hadn't made it to the kid? What if time had run out for both of them? Then what? He had risked it all and had been given a second chance. "I'm sorry. I should've never put you in that position."

"Me? You're apologizing for me?" she asked, jabbing a finger into her chest. "I'm a big girl, I can handle myself. What I chose to do on scene was my choice. I did it because I'm your friend. I'm your partner in the field. We have each other's backs because that's how it should be. No matter what, I would have followed you into that house. And I will continue to do so until the day I die."

It was his turn to raise a brow and look at her like she had just lost her mind. "I'd say that's a bit dramatic," he said, following up with a light chuckle.

"Say what you want to say, but it's the truth," she said, locking her eyes onto his. "It's how I feel and nothing will ever change that."

"Trust me when I say this, and believe me when I tell you it's not the alcohol," he joked. "But I feel the same way you do. There's nothing I wouldn't do for you. Or the squad. It's my job to protect you...and them."

Stumbling over his words wasn't pleasant. He hated how bad he wanted to tell her how he truly felt. It pained him to keep it from her for so long. A part of him knew there was a possibility she felt the same way about him, but the other part, the naysayer, told him he wasn't ready for a serious relationship anyway and she would laugh in his face with the thought of them being something more.

"I should let you get back to your movies," he said, pointing to the television. "I didn't mean to interrupt your fun tonight. I just figured now was a better time than later to talk to Adam about everything."

He stood to go, but she grabbed his arm and told him to wait. He sat back down and looked at her. The same pained expression crossed her face once again. He couldn't make out what that expression meant, but he knew she was troubled by something.

"Thank you for listening to me ramble," he said, offering her a smile, hoping it would ease her into saying something—anything—instead of looking at him like she had lost her voice. He couldn't help the panic he felt as he watched her, silently waiting for her to say what was on her mind.

"Conner," she said, keeping her eyes locked on his. "I've been wanting to tell you something for a long time and I think now is the time to tell you."

"Is this a joke? Like a play on my words from earlier?" he asked, laughing at the thought of her mocking him with an unknown fact about herself. "Are you going to tell me something I would have never guessed about you in a million years? Because if so, I'm sure I know everything there is to know..."

"I love you."

Tears welled in her eyes, a tremble brushed her lips, and her eyes resembled the panic he had felt when he thought about telling her the same exact thing. Except this time, he had no words. He needed to get out of there. It was late. He'd been drinking. Hell, he was still buzzed.

There was no way she had meant to say those three words that had an incredible impact on their life—on their friendship.

"I better get going," he said, standing abruptly from the couch as he reached into his pocket for his truck keys. Releasing the breath he had been holding, he made his way to the door. Turning back, he witnessed the pained expression on her face, but this time, it was outlined by tears streaming down her cheeks. "I'll see you later?"

Before she had time to say anything, he opened the door, exited the house, and ran to his truck. What the hell had just happened? What the hell were they going to do?

Climbing into his truck, he turned the key and the engine grumbled to life. He couldn't help but think of the pain he may have caused her by leaving the way he did. He would make it up to her, but not tonight. Tonight, he needed time to think and unwind. There was only one place he could do just that. And that was exactly where he was headed.

15

Watching Conner leave made her regret opening her mouth. She should have kept her mouth shut and her feelings to herself. It was obvious he didn't feel the same way about her, and what the hell had she been thinking telling him she loved him? Those three words were the only words that had the power to demolish their friendship, or what was left of it anyway.

Tossing her head back against the couch, she stared at the ceiling, recalling how stupid she had been tonight. Stupid feelings. Stupid mouth. Stupid emotions.

Now she was completely helpless, hopeless, and left fending for herself while reruns of Hallmark movies played on the television. The thought of calling Rosie crossed her mind, knowing her grandmother was most likely up at this hour anyway watching the same reruns Megan had been watching prior to being interrupted by Conner.

She knew she could count on her grandmother for advice and direction in handling this unforeseen circumstance. She also knew she would have to divulge everything to her grandmother, even though her grandmother most likely knew everything anyway.

Deciding against better judgment, she grabbed her phone and dialed Rosie's number. On the third ring, she answered.

"Meg? What's wrong? You never call at this hour," she said, sounding tired.

"I didn't wake you, did I?"

"No, dear, you didn't. Is everything okay?"

She hated to bother her over something so trivial and minute, but she was the best at settling doubts and giving the greatest advice. "Yes, I just needed to talk to someone, so I called you."

"Aww, Meg, you know I'm always here when you need me," her grandmother reassured. "What's going on? Are you all right?"

"I told Conner I loved him tonight," she said, releasing a shuddering breath. She inhaled deeply, awaiting her grandmother's response.

"And what did he say?"

"Nothing," Megan said, recalling the troubled memories from just a while ago. "He got up and left. He said he had to get going, but that was it."

"Oh, honey, I'm sure your words just caught him by surprise, is all," Rosie reassured her.

Megan knew it was more than likely the truth, but it was still hard to comprehend after watching him walk out the door with nothing to say. "You two have been the best of friends for so long, I'm sure he feels the same way you do. He just probably hasn't realized it yet."

Laughing at her grandmother's remark, Megan allowed herself to let go of some doubt while holding tight to what remained—hurt and betrayal. It still hurt that he had left her hanging, once again, in a time she needed him.

"You know what they say about men, right?" she asked, making sure Megan was still listening. "It takes them a while to come around, to catch onto something right in front of them," Rosie said, laughing into the phone. "Do you remember how long it took Wes to come around after I told him how I felt about him? Granted, it had been a year since he had lost his wife, but still. It took him a long while to grasp what I was trying to tell him."

Her grandmother's laugh was music to her ears. It had been a long night, and to know that everything would most likely be okay relieved her from stressful doubts.

"What if what I said makes things awkward, though? What if he really doesn't feel that way? What if him leaving was my sign that he doesn't feel the way I do?"

"Honey, relax," Rosie said into the phone. "You're overthinking it. More than likely he feels the same way you do and he got scared at the change it entails, so he left. It was too much for him to take on, which meant the only option he had was to get the hell out of there before he said something he would later regret."

"I don't know. I want to think you're right, but at the same time, his actions spoke louder than his words. Well, especially since he didn't say any."

Him leaving would haunt her thoughts until he justified it with a reason worth the hurt and the other emotions it had awakened inside of her. It wasn't fair that he had left, but it also wasn't fair that she had thrown those three simple, but life-changing words at him. What the hell had she been thinking?

"Even if he doesn't feel the same way you do, you have nothing to lose," Rosie said, and for a minute, Megan was confused. How did she have nothing to lose? Conner unfriending her and leaving her just because of her feelings meant the end of her hopes and dreams. It sounded dramatic, sure, but she only knew of life with him, not without him. It seemed daunting and impossible to think of life without him near her. "I mean, you'll still be friends and you'll still have him in your life. I promise, things won't be as horrible as you're thinking they'll be."

"I wish I knew that for sure," Megan said, doubt filling her thoughts once again. "I just wish he would've said something, anything, to let me know how he feels. But instead, he left and took my heart with him."

"Trust the love you feel and go with it," Rosie assured her. "In time, he'll come around and I promise you'll know if it's worth it. Even now, if the love you have for him is worth it, you'll stick it out and travel the rough waters. You'll know in time how he feels without him even having to say a single word. All relationships take work and don't start off perfect like those movies we watch."

Chuckling at her grandmother's witty remark about Hallmark movies, Megan decided she had a point. Love was worth the wait. If he felt the same way she did, he would tell her in time. She had to be patient and wait. He was going through a lot, and to be honest, it wasn't fair on her part to throw those words at him tonight. She should've waited until a better time, a time when he didn't have the world on his shoulders and a million things to sort out.

"Can I say just one more thing before you let me go?" her grandmother asked, and for a minute, Megan was hesitant to hear what her grandmother had to say. "Conner is a good guy, and sometimes, even when they have the best intentions, they end up hurting the ones they love without truly meaning to. Don't give up on him, Megan. Trust love will find its way and things will work out."

"Thanks, Grandma," Megan said, feeling much better now than when she first picked up the phone. "Good night, love you."

Hanging up the phone, she decided to call it a night. The kids would be waking up early and they would be requesting breakfast. If she stayed up any longer, she'd need twice the amount of coffee on a regular day.

16

Levy's was packed for a weeknight, but that wouldn't stop Conner from venturing inside and tipping back a few. It had been a helluva week already and knowing Megan felt the same way he did, he should be happy and on top of the world, but that was not the case.

The friendship shared between them was worth too much for them to throw it all away if things didn't work out. He wasn't afraid of falling deeper in love with her. Hell, there really was no way to love her more than he already did.

"So what's the latest on you two?" Liam asked, sliding a mixed drink in front of him, pointing over to Megan, who had been ignoring him since he got there. It'd been a couple of days since she'd spilled her feelings to him. For one reason or another, he couldn't justify his reason for leaving. Had he been surprised by her confession? Of course. Happy? Damn straight. Scared? Hell yes.

The fact Liam was onto something between them had started long before his coming back to Cedar Valley. Adam had informed Conner once the word got out that he was coming back from Colorado, Megan's eyes had lit up and her concern of his arrival was all she cared about.

It was funny looking back on all of that now. He had thought she only cared because she was getting her best friend back—the same one who ditched her and the same one who hadn't been acting right since his return. Megan should hate him for how he'd been acting, but instead, she refused to give up on him.

"I don't know, man." Conner tipped back his drink, glancing over in Megan's direction. Swirling the amber liquid and ice before catching another glance in her direction, Conner said, "I had no idea she felt that way. As a friend, yeah, but we're not in that stage anymore."

Liam laughed, swiping Conner another refill. "You're definitely *not* in that stage anymore," he said, full of reassurance. "What are you going to do about it? She's probably waiting for the other shoe to drop since you left her hanging at Adam's place."

Conner knew it had been foolish of him to walk out and leave her on the couch. If he could do it all over again, he would have never left her. Instead, he would have...

"Hey," he called out to her as she made her way around their end of the bar. When she ignored him, he reached out to grab her attention, but she shrugged away from him, never once looking his way. "Dammit."

Liam laughed, throwing a towel over his shoulder. "She's a tough one," he said with a shit-eating grin across his face. "Which I'm sure you already know that."

Conner had no choice but to sit it out and wait. Drinking every night wasn't going to help him in the long run, especially since he was on his last chance with Adam and the department, but what the hell did that guy know about coping with bullshit? He didn't. He hadn't lost friends in a fire as he stood back and watched, trying desperately to put out the flames only to watch them sway and jump, mocking the men with the hoses. Adam didn't know what it was like because he hadn't left Cedar Valley. He hadn't left and struck out on a once in a lifetime opportunity. He didn't have to worry about hiding his pain, or getting through the day. Hell, he had a beautiful fiancée, two happy-go-lucky kids, and a home to call his own.

"Grab me another, please," Conner demanded, slamming his empty glass on the counter. "I can't handle this shit."

"Hey, if it helps, I've been there," Liam said, admitting something Conner would have never guessed. Liam was the grandson to a Spencer. He had his life made for him. What the hell had he been through where he understood where Conner was sitting at now? Hell, the Spencers and Jacobsens went way back. So far back, this town was damned near built on their namesake alone. "Not exactly proud of it. No one knows except my grandfather, and maybe a few others, but it happened and I understand where you're at."

"I'll bite," Conner said, taking a drink of the smooth amber liquid, this time drinking it slow because he knew Liam would likely cut him off soon. "What happened?"

He watched Liam's jaw tense, a look in his eyes dark and painful. He knew that look. He saw it every day in the mirror. Hell, that look became a permanent feature since that fateful day in Colorado.

"Not that my story compares to yours, but I know what it's like losing control of something and having to live with the aftermath every day," Liam explained, pulling up a seat next to Conner. "I hate to tell ya, though, throwin' those back ain't going to help you through it."

Conner eyed Liam's hand as it motioned to his mixed drink. He didn't need Liam to tell him what he already knew, but it was what it was and right now, drinking calmed the ache and filled the depressing hole gaping a mile wide in the center of him.

"Look, I think you should go talk to someone," Liam said, patting Conner on the back. The last thing Conner wanted to hear was a suggestion to go talk to someone—aka a damned therapist. "It'll only get worse until you do. Trust me."

Shaking his head, he tossed back the rest of his drink. "Nope, that isn't going to happen. I like my alcohol way too damn much and I ain't talkin' to a therapist. They wouldn't understand what I've been through. What I've seen."

"You're right, they won't," Liam agreed, keeping a firm grip on Conner's shoulder, a definite way to keep him grounded in his seat. "But that's not the point. The point is to get your mind cleared. Hell, you're lucky Adam hasn't pulled you off the squad."

Anger shot through Conner as he doubled his fist. Pounding the counter, he turned to Liam, who hadn't backed away—that man wasn't afraid of anything. "He's already tried. But I'm not going anywhere. This is my town too, and I'll be damned if some asshole is going to change that. Especially not Adam or my fucking father. Fuck them."

He'd drunk too much. He knew by the look on Liam's face he had said too much, but who the hell cared anymore? Not him, so what was the big deal?

"Look, I'm just saying you're in control of how this plays out. You're the one with the ability to change how things pan out around here," Liam said, offering Conner another firm grip on his shoulder. "I've been there, done that, and until Leah came into my life, I didn't understand what was at risk. You have to learn to let go and move on. You can't bring your friends back, and it sucks, but you can't let that screw your life up. Trust me."

Conner still wondered what the hell Liam knew about what it was like, but before he had a chance to ask him for a follow-up, Liam said, "I got in a really bad car accident when I first got my license. I thought I knew it all. I was young with a brand-new license in my hand."

Liam stood, scooting back the chair he had sat in the last half hour or so, and made his way back around the counter. It was obvious he was still uncomfortable talking about this even to this day. Conner listened intently, waiting for more of the story. He couldn't imagine where this story would end up or how it related to his own, but Liam was a good friend and good friends listened to each other. Which made his eyes wander over to Megan, who was still a pro at this ignoring game.

"I'd tried several times to pass that damn driving test and the day I finally did was the day no one could tell me anything," Liam continued with a white knuckled grip on the counter. "If they'd told me to take the corners slow, not to drive fast and reckless in the rain, I wouldn't have listened. If they'd told me, it wouldn't have mattered. It was all fun and games that night, until it wasn't fun anymore."

Liam tipped back a shot and slammed his glass on the counter. Conner took that time to take a drink himself.

"I was driving about sixty-five seventy miles an hour and came up on a curve too sharp to make going that fast. I'd traveled that road to school and back every day of my childhood, but yet had spaced that corner by our house," Liam said, anger twisting his face. More than likely the memories from that night flashed through his mind. "My buddy and I were just out for a cruise, listening to music and the windows rolled down. Rain was pouring, but we didn't care. There wasn't anyone there to tell us to roll up the damned windows. We were young, but we were adults once we owned that plastic card in our hands. I tried to slow down, but it was no use. The tires continued to spin as we flipped end over end."

Liam took a minute to collect his thoughts and grab Conner another drink, telling him it was his last one for the night, but he'd need to drink one with him just to hear the rest of this gruesome story.

"All I remember is yelling at my friend, seeing grass and dirt, a few trees here and there as my head bounced around." Liam shook his head. "Hell, there was some point I'd lost consciousness because I don't remember shit at certain points, but what I do remember was looking over in the passenger seat for my buddy and he wasn't there. I could hear the sirens screeching in the background, a deafening the noise in my head, but I was in complete panic wondering where the hell my friend was."

Conner listened on, not moving a muscle. This story didn't compare at all to his own, but it was a hell of one.

"Rescue crews got there, worked on getting me out of the smashed up Trans Am and no sooner than I was cleared, I yelled for my buddy, but they didn't tell me anything," Liam said, looking down at his half empty glass as he sloshed the ice around. "It wasn't until the next day when my parents and grandfather came into my hospital room that I learned of my friend's death. A death that could've been prevented. If only I had listened to the advice of others. If only I hadn't been so young and dumb."

Pouring another refill for himself, Liam looked up, catching Conner's eyes with his. A painful expression filled his eyes, and when Conner wouldn't have continued on with the story, his friend did. "He was ejected out of the passenger seat. There was enough force as the car rolled, to toss him out like a ragdoll and smother him when it finally came to a stop." Choking on his words, Liam took a minute to catch himself. "I couldn't see my friend because the car was on top of him. And I couldn't see him at the funeral for one last time because the accident had made him unrecognizable. That's something I'll never forgive myself for, but I've lived with it because of the help I've gotten from a therapist."

Conner nodded. He needed help with it, and Liam was right. Only he was in control of how this life panned out for him. Sure, his brother had told him one last chance, and the drinking had to stop or he'd be kicked off the service for good, but right now, he wasn't sure of anything except one thing—he was numb and the pain was gone, leaving him empty and feeling good.

17

Seeing Conner walk into the bar and sit there with subtle glances her way had her heart beating out of her chest. She hadn't seen him since the night at Adam's. The night she had said those three delicate words and changed their world forever.

Having mixed feelings about whether to talk to him or keep ignoring him, she chose the latter and felt the shift in her world the instant she made the decision not to pay attention to him.

She could feel his presence linger around her. She could feel his eyes bore into her while she refused to look up from her distraction. A part of her wanted to ask him what the hell he was doing here, especially after catching wind about Adam warning him to stop drinking. That whole conflict in and of itself was overwhelming. Conner had made it apparent he wasn't going to stop drinking and what he chose to do on his own time was none of Adam's concern.

Everything was spiraling out of control for Conner and he was either waiting in anticipation for something to happen, or he was ignoring all signs that something was about to go wrong. She wanted to grab a hold of him and shake him until he realized the kind of fire he was playing with when it came right down to it.

Watching Liam take a seat next to Conner, she pretended not to pay attention, but she couldn't help to eavesdrop on what they were saying. It really wasn't her business, but it involved her best friend and she cared too much to ignore it.

Liam's confession caught her by surprise and some things a person was unable to unhear. That was one of those things. She had been a family friend since she was in her teens, and Rosie had been seeing his grandfather for what seemed like forever, there had been no talk whatsoever about Liam's car accident and killing his friend.

Wiping down the tables, waiting for the guys to call it a night, she occupied herself for the time being. It was getting late, and most of the patrons had long since left once the clock struck midnight, a regular occurrence on a weeknight —people usually didn't hang around till closing.

It hadn't taken long, only a few tables and a couple of booths wiped down, before Conner stood and with Liam's assistance, made his way to the door that would lead him to the upstairs loft. She was more than thankful Conner had taken her advice and moved in up there, and that Liam allowed him to. Especially on nights like tonight, where the last thing she wanted was for him to leave Levy's with an over the limit blood alcohol limit.

She saw Conner turn, taking one last look over at her before making his way out the door. She wanted so badly to say something to him, to hug him and tell him how sorry she was for saying those damned words. Tell him how much she regretted saying them and wanted things to go back to normal between them—however normal they could get. But instead, she waited until she heard a click and released the breath she had been holding.

Liam called out to her, waving her over to the counter. Motioning for her to have a seat, he slid a chair out for her and sat down across the way. Not sure what to say, she waited a minute or two for him to say something first. She wasn't sure how she truly felt about Liam knowing everything, but he was a good friend, damned near family, and if she was going to tell anyone besides Rosie, she would tell Liam.

She would have told Rachel, but that would have been awkward with Conner and Adam's feud. She just assumed to keep Rachel and Adam out of this mess until she figured things out. That's where Liam came in.

"That was deep," he said, running a calm hand through his hair. He stood, walked over to the cooler, and grabbed a couple bottles of water. He was back and sitting down by her, offering her one before she had a chance to say no thanks. But it'd been a long night. She was thirsty and water would have to do. She'd seen too much alcohol drinking tonight to even want a drink. What she wanted more than anything else right now was to call it a night, go home, crawl into bed after a hot shower, and sleep away the constant thought of how messed up she had made things.

"Hey, are you okay?" Liam asked, leaning forward as he waved a hand in front of her face. "It's been a long night. Do you want to go on home? I can finish closing up."

"No, I think I'll sit here for a minute," she said, taking the remaining energy she had just to offer a slight smile.

"Do you wanna talk about it?"

She hesitated, knowing it wouldn't change things between her and Conner if she talked about it with others, but also knowing it would do her good to get things off her chest. Her feelings were conflicted and if she were honest, this was one situation she had lost control over and it bothered her to admit it.

"Can you tell me what goes through a guy's mind when he hears those three words?" she asked, laughing at how silly the question was to be asking a man who was well established and sitting good in life. He had a wife, a beautiful little girl, and another on the way. He obviously hadn't run when Leah had said those words to him, so he couldn't possibly answer her question the right way. The only one who could do that was upstairs, hopefully sleeping off the booze from tonight.

"Well, to be honest," Liam said, unscrewing the lid off his bottle of water before taking a quick drink. "It's definitely scary to hear those words for the first time."

"You? Scared? Yeah, right," she teased, but in all seriousness, she couldn't believe it. Liam and Leah were the prime example of love at first sight and knowing it was right from the beginning. She couldn't believe he would have thought to be scared off by those words.

"No, seriously," he said, straight-faced without a flinch. "When Leah first said those words to me, I can remember my heart racing out of my chest and my palms got real sweaty. I'd known she felt that way, but to hear her actually say those words...man, I couldn't believe it."

"You've definitely got yourself a keeper," Megan said, smiling at the thought of his happy little family—the perfect picture of what family was all about.

"I guess what I felt most was panic. I couldn't wrap my head around her saying those words and actually meaning them," Liam said, brushing off his confession with a slight chuckle. "Of all things to be panicked about, her saying those words trumped the list. A woman like her with a guy like me. The man upstairs had a lot to do with that combination, that's for sure."

"Not Conner," Liam quickly corrected, waiting for her to laugh along with him. "I think it's common for all guys to have a moment of panic after hearing those words. If they don't, then they saw 'em coming from a mile away."

"Conner definitely didn't see them coming, that's for sure," she admitted, knowing she had blindsided him with what she had said, no warning it was coming. A complete whammy he wasn't ready for. "I just wish he would have said something. Anything would have been better said than nothing at all."

"Not to make excuses for him, but he's still young and dumb," Liam said, drinking the rest of his water. "He most likely feels the same way you do and it shocked him to hear you say it first."

"But what if he doesn't feel the same way?" She couldn't help but feel the doubt creeping back in. If there was anything she had learned in the last week, it was the fact she didn't take rejection or confrontation too well. And having Conner walk out the door without saying a word to her, it felt incomplete and made her feel rejected to say the least. "What am I supposed to do? Sweep my feelings under a rug and pretend I never said anything? But I did, and I'm not sure I can just brush them away and forget about my love for him."

Liam's eyes were locked on hers. She had him thinking, which was good, because she needed answers. She needed advice on how to avoid being hurt more than she already was. If he had anything to offer, she would gladly accept his advice. Especially if that advice was to forget it ever happened and go on with her life.

"I can't tell you what to do, but I can tell you to wait it out. Let him come around," he suggested, "come to his senses if you will."

She couldn't help agreeing with the last part. Conner had a long ways to go in order to come to his senses, and she hoped it was sooner rather than later. "You think he ever will?"

"I don't know."

Maybe it was best if she just walked away, forgetting what was said and how she felt. This whole caring too much was her weakness, and not only did she care too much about Conner, she cared too much about everything, including what he was thinking about her now.

"But what I do know is he has a lot on his plate and he's trying his hardest to do things right," Liam stated, tossing the empty bottle into a nearby trashcan. "I say just give him some time and he'll come around. But do me a favor and don't ignore him anymore. That poor guy kept watching you with sad eyes, waiting for you to say something to him."

"Good, the feeling's mutual then."

She hated to play the cards this way, but she had no other choice in the matter. She had been hurt and the ball was in his court. Waiting for him to come around could take forever and she didn't know if she wanted to wait that long for him to say something. For now, she would pretend nothing had been said. She would continue to ignore him until he made a move. The worst that could happen would be him moving on and forgetting it really did happen.

18

Stumbling out of bed, he grabbed his clothes and hurried out the door. He had ten minutes to get to the station for his shift. Struggling into his pants, he realized it had been dumb to go to Levy's last night. What the hell had he been thinking to drink that much before a shift the next day?

Sliding the door open, he scrambled down the stairs and out the back door as he fumbled for his keys in his pants pocket. Hopping into his truck, he tapped his watch and realized he wasn't going to make it in time. *Shit.*

Backing out of his parking spot, he threw the truck in drive and raced to the station. He had less than a minute to make it inside without Adam noticing how late he actually was.

Shifting into park, he killed the engine, grabbed his shirt, and tossed it over his muscle shirt on his way inside. Newbie greeted him, but Conner didn't have time for pleasantries. If he wanted to keep his job, he needed to get his shit together and make it to the back room before...

"Where've you been?" Adam called out from behind him as he shuffled past the office, trying hard not to be seen yet. Too late. "Conner."

Turning around, he regretted his late night decision once he saw the look on his brother's face. This was it. The last chance he had been given, he had just blown it. He'd seen that look before and knew what was coming next. He held his spot and waited for that shoe to drop.

"Are you still drunk?" The accusation echoed in the hallway, causing Conner to cringe. "Answer me, Conner. Are you still drunk?"

Conner felt his insides mangle at his brother's tone. He hated that his issues had come to this. He wanted nothing more than to give this service everything he had to give, but instead, he was wreaking havoc every chance he got. Disappointment crossed Adam's face followed by a second's frustration.

"My office, now," Adam said, pointing Conner in the direction of the open door. As he walked by Adam and into his office, he could hear Adam taking whiffs of him. Knowing he was busted red-handed, he turned and faced Adam.

"Look, I can explain," he said, trying his damnedest to get Adam to give him just one more chance—anything to prove he was better than this. He'd gotten off on the wrong foot. His talk with Liam last night had sunk in and he realized he needed to reach out for help and actually follow through with it this time.

"There's no need to explain," Adam said, pulling his chair up to his desk. He pulled out Conner's file from the cabinet and wrote something in scribbles along the bottom. "It's perfectly clear where we stand in this matter and I've given you several chances to get your shit together. I don't know what else I can do for you. I can't keep giving you chances just to blow 'em without a care in the world. Look at you."

It hurt to not only see the disappointment on his brother's face, but to hear in it in his voice too. He really messed up this time. He wondered if not showing up at all today would have been a better option. Hell, he'd still be facing the consequences of his never-ending bad decision-making skills.

"Do you have any idea how ridiculous you look right now?" Adam asked, jabbing a finger in Conner's direction. "What? Did you honestly think I wouldn't see how drunk you are after last night's bender? Or that I wouldn't be able to smell the alcohol on you?"

Conner said nothing. He sat still, waiting silently for the shoe to drop. For his brother to toss him out the door without another word spoken.

"Did you even take a shower?"

Shaking his head, embarrassed that his actions had led to this moment, he kept his eyes on the floor.

"You leave me no choice, Conner," Adam said, signing another paper before looking up at Conner. "You can either resign from your position here, or I fire you. Either way, you are no longer welcome to run on my squad."

This was really it. This was where everything he had worked so hard for came crashing down around him. Everything he had tried to do for the better had gone completely wrong and here he was, two seconds from being jobless—a professional death he never thought twice about because he knew it would never happen to him. Boy, had he been wrong. Hell, he'd been wrong about a lot of things lately.

Fighting back the anger, the rage that built up inside of him, he nodded at his brother's suggestion to resign. He wouldn't resign. If his brother wanted him off the service, he would have to fire him, otherwise he wasn't going anywhere.

"What's it going to be?" Adam asked, tapping the pen against the papers he had been busy signing minutes ago. "If you choose to resign, I'll need a written statement from you by day's end. Otherwise..."

Grunting, Conner shifted in his chair. He couldn't believe his brother was treating him like this. He couldn't believe this was how things were going to be. He had two choices, but he didn't want to take either of them. He wanted to go back home and come back tomorrow with a clear head. Give Adam a chance to chill out and think about what he was doing before he actually did it.

The fear he felt when he lost his friends, when Megan had said those three words, when he almost lost his life... that fear couldn't compare to the fear he felt right now. He was about to lose his job, his career, everything he had worked so hard to get. It was all crumbling around him.

"If you want me gone, you'll have to fire me," he said, spitting words at Adam from across the desk. "I don't believe you would actually fire me."

Adam stood, dropping his pen on his desk, and leaned over to come face-to-face with Conner. "I guess you better believe it because you're fired. Get your shit and get out of here."

"You'll regret this," Conner said, making his way to the door. "You'll wish you had never let me go. You're my fucking brother, for Christ's sake!"

"The only one who's going to regret anything is you,"

Adam said, ushering him out of his office. "Get your shit together, Conner, before you end up messing your life up."

Conner couldn't believe this was happening. His own brother of all people was kicking him off the service. What the hell was he going to do now?

19

Feeling refreshed after her talk with Liam and having a day off to do absolutely nothing while she binge watched Netflix, Megan was anxious to get back to work. She had no idea what would happen between her and Conner, but she was more than ready to get it over with. Whatever would happen, would happen. It was out of her control and she didn't have a clue where to go from here.

Pulling out of her driveway, she headed east to the fire station, not realizing she had gotten ready in record time this morning and had at least thirty minutes to spare before her shift started.

Taking it as an opportunity to grab breakfast, she whipped a U-turn and headed toward the café. She would grab Conner breakfast too—a way for her to let him know things were still cool between them, even though they were far from that.

"Good morning, Meg," Granny Mae called out to her as soon as the bell rang above the door as she stepped inside. "How are you doing on this fine day?"

Granny Mae had been the reason why her grandmother was out of the house and doing so well after her stroke. Giving her grandmother something to focus on besides the setbacks from having a stroke, Granny Mae had offered her part ownership of this diner and so far, it seemed to work out for them.

"Well, I'm doing well, actually," Megan said, pulling up a seat at the counter. "I have a bit before shift starts, so I figured I'd stop and grab some breakfast."

"Sounds like a good idea to me," Granny Mae said, patting Megan's hand before grabbing her pen and pad of paper out of her apron's pocket. "What can I get you?"

Megan glanced at the menu scrawled on the chalkboard hanging right behind Granny Mae. Biscuits, gravy, and a side of either bacon or sausage, along with a side of scrambled eggs. "I'll have what's on the board times two, please," Megan said, pointing to the board and smiling when Granny Mae made a face as though she knew who the other breakfast plate would be for.

"You've gotta date going on when you get to work, do ya?" Granny Mae winked, but her words were enough to make Megan smile while her cheeks blushed. It was funny a man could have that much control over her reactions. Not just any man, but Conner. "I'll get those right out to you so you won't be late."

She watched Granny Mae wink and laugh on her way to the kitchen. As soon as Granny Mae cleared the doorway, Rachel walked out and smiled at Megan. She walked up to the counter and grabbed a seat next to her.

"How are things going?" Rachel asked, turning sideways in her chair in order to face Megan's side.

"Pretty good."

She had no choice but to keep her thoughts secret from

Rachel. Not that she didn't trust Rachel. It was just a complicated mess of sorts and involving Rachel would somehow involve Adam, and Megan wasn't ready for others' opinions flying at her when she had no idea what the outcome of this whole situation would be.

"That's good. I'm so thankful you watched the kids for us," she said, keeping the conversation light and happy between them.

Megan guessed Rachel had heard about Conner and everything that had been happening lately with him and the service. She just wished he would get his shit together. Hopefully after his talk with Liam the other night, he would get his act together.

"It's been forever since Adam and I have been able to have a night away."

Rachel had given her the scoop on their final destination and where they had eaten supper and stayed overnight at the next morning when they came back home. The kids had been super excited to see their parents were home, but more sad to see Megan leave. She had promised to watch them more often. They had made watching them a piece of cake.

"I'll have to watch them again sometime soon," Megan said, smiling as Rachel's face lit up.

"They would love that," Rachel said, excited with the thought of making her kids happy. The saying was most likely true about when mama's happy, everyone's happy. It was apparent by the look on Rachel's face. "We would love that too."

Rachel brought Megan in for a hug and once again said how thankful she was to have met her and have become good friends. It was still weird for Megan to have female friends. She had never been one of those girly girls who liked to shop and get nails done—yeah, once in a while, but not like some of the girls in her school. She'd rather spend time on the farm, rounding up horses or cattle, getting them ready for shows and selling them. Maybe that was why she and Conner had become such good friends. They'd had a lot in common while growing up. It was a good thing they'd had each other.

"I better get back in the kitchen before my cupcakes burn," Rachel said, hopping off the chair and heading toward the kitchen door just as Granny Mae brought two to-go boxes out and set them on the counter in front of Megan. When Megan reached into her wallet to pay, Granny Mae tapped her hand and shook her head. "It's my treat. Have a good breakfast date with whoever that special someone may be."

"Thank you, Granny," Megan said, smiling from ear to ear. She grabbed the boxes and took off out the front door.

She hoped Conner was there a bit early so they could eat breakfast together.

Parking in her favorite spot, she climbed out of her car and made her way inside. The smell of the food inside the boxes had her stomach rumbling on the way over to the station. Now, she was just minutes from scarfing down.

First glance showed no sign of Conner. It was possible he was in the back room getting his uniform on, like he had done several times before when he was running behind and wore his street clothes in from home.

"Hey, Chase," she called out on her way by the lounge area. "How's it goin'?"

He was on his feet in no time, following her to the kitchen. "It's going. What'd you bring me for breakfast?"

The kid was definitely a newbie. He was younger than Conner and had a lot to learn around here, starting with finding his own food in the mornings. Laughing, she shook her head and pushed him back away from the food. "I didn't get you anything," she said with a slight chuckle. Realizing how bitchy she sounded, she smiled. "Because I didn't know you were going to be here. Speaking of which, have you seen Conner yet this morning?"

The deer in the headlights look never got old, but right now, it was the last thing she wanted to see when asking about Conner. "You haven't heard?"

Her heart sank while a thousand thoughts raced through her mind on what that could possibly mean in regards to Conner. "Heard what?" She silently prayed for him to be okay.

"Adam let him go yesterday," Chase said as he leaned against the counter.

"Let him go? What do you mean let him go?"

Chase shrugged and she wanted to shake the answer out of him. "They had a huge blowout in the office yesterday right after Conner showed up. Something about still being drunk and a disappointment to this service and family."

"Shit."

Tossing the boxes into the fridge, she turned back to Chase and asked, "Where's Adam? I gotta go talk to him."

"In his office. He—"

She cut him off and headed for Adam's office down the hall. There was no way any of this had happened when she hadn't been here. She hadn't heard a single word about it, so the possibility of it not happening was still there. Shoving open his office door, she made her way in and stood across from him. Emotional rage was racing through her blood and she knew she needed to cool it or this wouldn't end well for her.

"Is there something I can help you with, Meg?"

She held up her hand, giving him a fierce look. "Cut the crap, Adam. What the hell happened yesterday? Did you really let him go?"

"I didn't have a choice."

Anger burned through her body and she wanted nothing more than a damn reason why Adam of all people would kick his own brother off the squad. She wanted answers, not excuses or beating around the bush. She wanted to know what the hell had happened and why it had come down to kicking Conner out of here. It was the last thing she had expected Adam to do, and the last thing Conner needed in his life right now.

"Are you sure about that?" Megan asked, fully aware she was crossing the line, but that line didn't matter right now. What mattered was Conner and Conner wasn't here because his brother had "no choice" to let him go.

"Megan, watch your tone," Adam warned, standing from his chair. "He left me no choice but to kick him off the squad. He had a choice to resign or be fired. He chose the latter. Hell, he had plenty of chances to do right around here and he kept messing up. It's not my fault he couldn't handle the responsibility."

Megan shook her head. She knew better. Conner wasn't the greatest at making good decisions, but he loved this department, he loved being a firefighter. Anything he had done wasn't intentional and the last thing he had wanted was to mess up so bad he'd lose his job. She now worried about where he'd gone and where he could possibly be by now. She silently prayed he hadn't left Cedar Valley.

"I don't know why you're such a hard-ass on him," Megan said, definitely crossing that line. "You think he doesn't have enough going on? You think you needed to fight with him and make things more difficult? Just to what? Prove you're in charge?"

"Megan, this is your final warning," Adam said, holding up a hand in an attempt to make her stop, but it wouldn't stop her. She was pissed and she had every right to be. Her best friend was out there somewhere without a job and nowhere to go. His own family was full of shit.

"What'd he do *so* wrong this time that you had *no choice* but to let him go?" Her breathing was erratic and her emotions were all over the place. She hated Adam and didn't want to be here having this conversation. She wanted to be out looking for Conner.

"He showed up for his shift still drunk," Adam said, sighing as he said the words, as though his disappointment was heavier than the issue at hand. She didn't care about Adam's disappointment. She didn't care how pissed he and his dad had been at Conner. Conner didn't deserve to be treated like a stray dog no one wanted. He deserved someone to care about him, to tell him they were there for him. Instead, all he got was a kick in the ass and was shoved out of the way, out of their hair.

She stopped her thoughts and heard Adam's words. She couldn't process them. "Drunk?"

"Drunk." Adam crossed his arms and waited for her to grasp the word and what it meant. "So drunk, in fact, that I could've gotten drunk by the fumes lingering on him when he stumbled in yesterday."

Adam had every right to do what he had done, but it

didn't seem fair. She needed to find Conner. She needed to make sure he was okay. She couldn't be here for one more second while she processed this whole mess from hell. "I've gotta go find him. I need to make sure he's okay. He needs help, Adam. He loved this job more than life itself."

Adam nodded, and without sticking around for another minute, she raced out of his office and to her car. She grabbed her phone and dialed Conner's number but wasn't surprised when it went straight to voicemail.

20

With nowhere to go, Conner locked himself in the loft, away from noise and people. He was in no mood to deal with it. He had stocked up on booze yesterday, stuffing the fridge to the brim with nothing but alcohol, and it felt damn good.

He had tried to call his dad to talk to him, but to no surprise of his own, his dad refused to talk. The fight between them had gone on far too long and it seemed almost too ridiculous that it had come to this.

His parents were supposed to love him and offer support when he could no longer support himself, and to be honest, that was a long time ago. Two years and counting he had been messed up and struggling with coping. Now, everything crumbled around him, giving him one more reason to let loose, have fun, and drown himself in alcohol.

Turning his phone on, just to check if anyone cared enough to call, he was shocked to see voicemails pop up one right after the other. He knew Megan would be calling him sooner or later, so to hear her voice on the other end of the line was no surprise. The fact she had left so many messages since this morning meant she wasn't going to give up. More than likely, she was out looking for him. Which meant he should get up off this worn out couch and figure out his next spot to hide out.

He stumbled off the couch, pulled shorts on, and grabbed his keys. Shame on him for wanting to drive after having a bit too much to drink, but he didn't have far to go. The place he called his sanctuary was just down the way on a gravel road about two miles out of town.

Opening the door, he escaped the loft and made it to his truck without anyone noticing him. So far, so good. He wasn't ready for anyone to see him. He would come around eventually, most likely when he was ready to say goodbye before heading out west once again. He was a sucker for punishment and heading back to Colorado, no matter how sweet the view, it would be a bittersweet return for him.

Allowing the truck to idle for a few minutes, he collected his thoughts on where he was heading and why he wanted to go there. His grandparents would allow him in with wide-open arms and a smile on their face. Counting on them when things went south for him was something he knew he could do no matter what.

Now, knowing for sure where he was heading, he shifted into drive and headed down the road. Heading down the most familiar road to him in the whole county, he allowed it to guide him to the place he loved the most.

What he didn't realize when climbing into the truck was the fact he was doing exactly what *they* would think he had done—what he had done every chance he was given. He was running from his problems and refusing to face them.

A few minutes later, he pulled into the long drawn-out driveway that led him to his destination. Pulling in, he saw his grandma's car parked right in front of the garage. He pulled his truck out of sight from the road and killed the engine. As far as he was concerned, he would be here until he overstayed his welcome, which would never happen. His grandparents were closer to parents than his own, except he had to hand it to his mother, she was going through hell with his father and the ongoing conflicts, and she still hadn't given up on trying to make everything right.

"Conner? Is that you?" his grandma called from the kitchen. She met him in the entryway as he stepped inside. "What's going on?"

Panic traced the lines of her face and he could only imagine what she was thinking. Something along the lines of *what the hell happened to you* or *you look like hell* came to mind.

"Do you and Gramps mind if I hang out around here for a while?" Desperation coated his words and he felt guilty for being there, standing in their entryway like a stray dog on a rainy night begging for shelter.

"Of course, for however long you need to," she said, no hesitation, but her words were heavy with concern as it crossed her face. "But first, I want you to eat something. Have a seat, please. I'll bring you something."

She motioned for him to take a seat at the dining room table. She pulled out his chair and he sat. It was her way of reiterating his earlier thought of looking like hell. She had to know he was three sheets to the wind, but closer to four by now. He laughed at his own thoughts.

"Your grandfather went out to Wes' this morning to help with the horses," she called out from the kitchen. The smell of food frying in the pan wafted in and assaulted his senses. "They're having to put Whiskey down. He unlocked his barn gate the other night and got hit. They said there'd been a chance he would've pulled through his injuries, but now it's not looking so good."

That was too bad. He knew how much those horses meant to that family. And how much money they were bringing in with Leah's riding lessons and shows she had been doing until she got pregnant again.

Putting Whiskey down. *Damn.* The irony in that statement wasn't lost on him. He knew eventually he would have to give up the alcohol. Hell, he might as well give up now that he was with his grandparents. They'd help him get through it.

"Here you go, dear," his grandma said, placing a plate full of eggs and bacon in front of him. Taking a slice of bacon, he said thank you and ate while his grandmother sat next to him, watching him like a hawk while trying to figure out why he was there. He'd tell her as soon as he was done eating. He'd worked up quite the appetite while drinking nonstop over the last day or so. Something he didn't think was possible, he had done. He didn't want to become an alcoholic, but it was clear he may have crossed that mark a long time ago. It pained him to think of it. How much control he had lost over himself and his actions.

Shaking his head to clear his thoughts, he shoveled in a scoop of scrambled eggs while his grandma watched him in silence. He liked it here already. The difference between here and everywhere else, there was no tension. No dirty looks. No disappointed faces. He was who he was and his grandparents didn't judge him or criticize him.

Clearing his plate, he stood, but was told to sit back down and relax while his grandma carried it to the sink. She was back with a pot of coffee and two mugs. "Coffee?"

He wasn't much of a coffee drinker, but anything

sounded good at the moment. Reaching out for the steaming cup, he thanked her once again.

He looked over at her while she did the morning crossword in the paper. She was acting like everything was fine and this was a normal occurrence. It wasn't. It was far from it, but his grandma wouldn't be the one to say it without him initiating the conversation.

"Thanks for letting me in," he said, making light of the situation, knowing it was past the point of laughing or crying about it. Either way, he was screwed and it was his grandparents who would be able to help him correct this awful mess.

"You're always welcome here, you know that," his grandma said, taking a sip of her coffee as she filled in one more line on the crossword. Four boxes across and five down. He was never one for those damn things. He could never figure out all the clues. But his grandma, she was something else when it came to those crosswords. She would sit down in the early morning and before too long, she'd have the whole damn thing done and be started on the next one.

"Things have gotten pretty bad," he said, clearing his throat as he leaned forward on the table.

"I figured as much," she said, not once taking her pencil off the paper. Her focus on the puzzle was driven not only from dedication to finish it, but to avoid pressuring him into saying what he didn't want to. He'd known her his whole life. She'd been respectful like that, unlike his father.

"Well, you and Gramps are the only two I know who won't judge me. You two are the only ones I trust to help me get through this," he admitted, folding his hands in front of him.

His grandma put the pencil down, reached out, and set

her hand on top of his. "We've raised five kids in our time. We've learned over time what works and what doesn't. Some take longer than others to figure that out. And, you have to admit, five kids gives a lot of practice."

"In more ways than one," Gramps said, making his way into the dining room from the front room.

Conner laughed, knowing his grandfather had the tendency to be perverted. That old man's mind was in the gutter three quarters of the time. Nothing new there.

"Say, what brings you out this way?"

His grandma glared his gramps' way, and his gramps caught on that it had been the wrong thing to ask. "Oh," he said, walking straight by them. "Don't mind me. I'm just going to grab a bite to eat."

"Adam kicked me off the squad."

It felt good to say it out loud. A final recognition that it had in fact happened and he was without a job.

Gramps stopped in his tracks, turned, and faced Conner. Shock? Probably not. Everyone knew the day would most likely come, they just didn't know when. The look was more of want to know more than a standpoint. A curious look. His grandma, on the other hand, leaned back in her chair and crossed her arms. There was no doubt she was ready to hear more.

"I've been messing up," he admitted, taking a drink of his coffee and setting the mug back down on the table before saying, "a lot."

"Everyone messes up every now and again," Gramps said, pulling out a chair for himself as he sat down.

"Not like I have, they haven't."

"Well, I'll tell ya what," Gramps said, leaning forward as he rested his elbows on the table. "They'd be fools not to let you come back. And even if they don't, you keep your head in the game and figure something else out."

"I was drinking the night before shift," Conner said, hating to admit it. "I must've had too much, because I was still drunk when I stumbled into work the next day."

No reaction. No disappointed expressions. No "what the hell were you thinking." Silence, followed by a nod. This was why he loved his grandparents.

"That was hard," he admitted, looking down at his shaking hands. As bad as he wanted a drink right now, he knew he needed to fight against the craving.

Gramps nodded, knowing exactly where he was coming from. His gramps had seen his fair share of alcohol in his life. Hell, the man had most likely overcome alcoholism himself. As they say, it runs in the family, and it sure did with the Jacobsens. But Conner wouldn't be the one to judge because he knew what it was like to be the odd one out—the one who'd been hit with the addiction gene.

"You'll get through this, Conner," Gramps said, making sure Conner knew he wasn't alone in this fight. "Grams and I will help you through this. You stay here however long you need to and when you're ready, we'll still be here to help. Tell us what you need and you've got it. Understood?"

Conner's eyes filled with tears. An overwhelming emotion of being accepted with all his flaws washed over him. Aside from Megan, his grandparents had been the only ones who accepted him—mess and all.

With everything telling him to get the hell out of town, he wasn't going to listen. He was going to stay right here. His love for Megan and this town, for his grandparents and his brother was too strong to let him leave.

21

"Have any of you seen Conner?" Megan asked, walking into Levy's. The thought that someone had to have seen him by now guided her mission. It'd been a couple of days and he hadn't returned her calls. She was close to panic, and the only thing that stopped her from freaking out was the fact she hadn't heard anything come across the scanner in regards to a bad accident or possible death. The thought of him driving drunk had crossed her mind several times over the last two days, but she'd been up and down all the roads in town and hadn't seen any sign of his truck.

The paramedic in her wanted to make sure he was safe and far from harm's reach, but she couldn't do that without knowing where the heck he had run off to.

"No, he hasn't been here since that first day after Adam kicked him off the squad," Liam said, concern etched on his face.

Frustration mixed with a wide range of other emotions. She couldn't just sit around and wait for him to come waltzing in like he'd done several times before. Conner had been good about doing that. Anytime they'd least expected him to show up, he'd show up out of the blue and acted like everything was perfectly fine and nothing ever happened. If only he would do that right now, she would be able to relax. She wanted to make sure he was okay.

"I've driven all over town and I haven't seen him," she told Liam, who was wiping down tables and chairs, getting ready for the lunch crowd to come in. "I have no idea how to get a hold of him or find him when I have no idea where he would be. I used to know all of his hideouts, but now that we're older, I don't have a clue. Except here, because, well," she said, pointing to the booze lining the shelves. "I hope he didn't go back to Colorado. I don't want him to leave town. I want him to stay here, Liam."

"I'm not sure where he'd end up," Liam said, setting a bottle of water in front of her. "I was hoping after our talk the other night, he would've sought help and got what he needed before things got worse. I guess that didn't go as planned, huh?"

Megan shook her head, grabbed the water, and said thanks before chugging it. She hadn't slept more than a few hours here and there. She was dog-tired, dehydrated, and hated that she didn't know where he was. She wanted nothing more than to find him, bring him home, and make sure he understood how much he meant to her, to everyone here in Cedar Valley. Whether or not he would believe it, she would have to tell him, because it was true. Even if all the people didn't care, she did. She cared. And that alone should be enough to help him. It should be enough to keep him safe. It should've been enough.

"Liam, where else would he go?"

Thinking of all the places he could possibly end up, Megan placed her head in her hands. Thoughts flooded her mind and she ruled out half of them, until she realized of all the places she had thought to look, she had missed the most obvious place. The place he would venture off to regardless of what was going on, regardless of how late it was, or how far the drive was. He would head to that place rain or shine just so he wouldn't have to face judgement or ridicule.

"Why didn't I think of this sooner?" she said aloud, standing from her seat and reaching for her keys. Liam looked at her with concern as he watched her hustle toward the door. "His grandparents' house, Liam! It's the only place he would go when things were going wrong! I have to go. Make sure you let everyone know I found him! I'll call you and let you know for sure when I do!"

She hurried out the door and scrambled into her car. Turning the key in the ignition, she thanked God for the last-minute thought that would lead her to her best friend. She would be able to hug him and tell him everything would be all right. She would tell him she was on his side no matter what—through thick and thin. There was no other place she would rather be than by his side for now and forever as long as he would allow her to be there with him.

KICKING HERSELF IN THE ASS FOR NOT THINKING OF checking Edward's first, she shifted into drive and headed out of town on the county road that would lead her to their gravel road. If she had thought of them right away, she wouldn't have worried so much. Granted, there was still a chance he wouldn't be there, but that chance was slim to none. The odds were in her favor.

Gravel crunched under her tires as she drove off the main highway and onto the path to his grandparents' house.

Saying a quick prayer, she prayed for him to be there and not be too damaged by the consequences of his actions.

Pulling into their driveway, she parked near the front door and hopped out. There was no sign of his truck, but that didn't mean he hadn't hidden it from everyone's sight who might be out looking for him.

Rapping her knuckles against the mahogany stained door, she waited impatiently for them to answer. The more she had time to think about this, the more she realized she shouldn't care so damn much. Her thoughts were like broken records, scratched and still attempting to play the same beaten song over and over again with no change in the outcome.

"Megan?" Conner's grandmother opened the door, inviting her to come in without hesitation. "If you're here for who I think you're here for, he's in the back room."

Megan sighed in relief and followed his grandmother through the house and into the back room. She saw him before he had a chance to see her, but he remained seated once his eyes locked on her. Apparently, he was tired of running.

"Hey," she said, grabbing a spot next to him on the couch.

His grandpa stood, patted her on the shoulder, and said, "We'll leave you two alone for a bit."

"Thanks," she whispered, waiting for Conner to react to her being there. He looked rough. Lines etched deep on his face, making him look older than he should look, and his eyes were red, which she assumed had been from either drinking or crying, or both.

"I've heard the bad news," she said, starting the conversation without beating around the bush. She hated when others did that with her, so she wouldn't do it to others.

"Well, I didn't hear anything actually. I went in for my shift and you weren't there. I brought you breakfast and Chase said you were let go."

Finally, a reaction crossed his face. It wasn't a pleasant reaction, but it was something. Anger sparked a need for him to talk. "Yeah, this whole situation is bullshit."

"What happened? Why'd you show up drunk?" Her tone was subtle, but he still took offense as he leaned forward, close enough they were only inches apart and she couldn't help noticing the tension and heat between them.

"I wasn't drunk," he argued, scrubbing his hands through his hair. He definitely looked rough. "I quit drinking when you saw me leave the bar. I didn't have anything to drink past that time, whatever time it was."

"He says you were drunk. So drunk that he could've gotten drunk on your fumes," she explained, knowing he wasn't wanting to discuss it, but she wanted to get to the bottom of it. She wanted to make sure it really happened and this wasn't just a squabble between two bullheaded siblings. "Is it true that you were that drunk?"

He shrugged and she knew right then and there that it was most likely true and there was no way he could deny the facts. She wasn't one to judge, and she wouldn't start now. Everyone made mistakes. They were human and it was expected for them to mess up every now and then.

"If you're on his side, you can leave. I don't want to hear how bad I fucked up," he said, his face knotted in anger as he spat out the words. "Trust me, I already know I'm a failure."

"I'm not on his side. I'm on yours. If you haven't noticed, I came looking for you. If I were on his side, I wouldn't have spent countless hours looking for you. I wouldn't have lost sleep," she said, her voice cracking with emotion she shrugged off, getting pissed she had no control over the tears welling up in her eyes. "I wouldn't have worried about you driving off the road and killing yourself over something not worth it. I wouldn't be here right now. I wouldn't have cared."

His arms found their way around her, pulling her into his chest, a familiar gesture she had once been so used to, but now, she hadn't expected it. It felt good to be in his arms again. "Hey, don't cry. Not over me. I'm fine."

"I know that now," she said, her words muffled by his shirt. "I thought I lost you for good this time. It scared me. I hate that you ran off. I hate that you think everything would be better without you around. I hate that I care so damn much."

"Look, I'm sorry," Conner said, pulling back to look her in the eyes. "I shouldn't have left. I should've never left Cedar Valley ever, but I can't change the past. And up until recently, I thought I could make things right, but dammit, things didn't go my way and I ended up messing everything up. I messed up our friendship when I first left for Colorado, but lately, I've messed up my life by not knowing how to cope."

She was happy to hear his realization on how messed up things had gotten. How out of control things were now and why. What she didn't hear were his feelings about her. Shaking off those thoughts, she pulled out of his grasp and readjusted so they had space between them once again. She wasn't here to discuss feelings. She was here to make sure he was okay, and from the look of it, he was.

"I'm glad you're okay," she said. "That's all that matters. What happened, happened, and I'm not sure what you're going to do next, but I'm sure you'll figure it out. You always do."

The anger and frustration in her voice was apparent. It was his chance to tell her what his plans were, or what thoughts he had, but he remained silent. Nothing felt more like a waste of time than this very moment. Either he didn't care at all, or he wasn't ready to talk about it. Either way, she wasn't going to sit around and let her emotions take over.

"I've gotta get going," she said, trying to make a run for it before her emotions got the best of her. "I went looking for you and I've found you. You're safe and in good hands, so my work here is done."

She stood up, wanting so bad to stay there, to keep talking to him, but it was obvious he wasn't up to talking more than he'd already done.

"Wait, Meg," he said, standing from his spot on the couch. "I'll get this figured out. Thanks for checking on me."

"Yeah, no problem." She grabbed her keys and made her way to the door. Turning back to face him, she said, "I guess I'll see you around?"

He nodded, which was far from what she was expecting, but it was what it was and she decided it was her cue to leave.

22

Watching Megan leave was hard, but he needed to call Adam and meet up with him. She was the last person he wanted to witness their conversation. More than likely, it wouldn't be good and things wouldn't end well. She had been in the middle of all this for quite some time now and had risked her life and even her job to stand up for him when he didn't deserve it.

It was time to make amends. He and Gramps had a conversation late into the morning hours about doing the right thing and owning up to mistakes when mistakes were made. It didn't get more simple than that. Hell, there was nothing simple about it, because everything they talked about was easier said than done. He was sure Adam wouldn't want to hear from him, now or ever. Most likely, Adam and their father had drinks while discussing how big of a joke Conner was. That was a laughable thought. At least they'd have something to talk about. It wouldn't be the first time and it definitely wouldn't be the last.

"Hey, Grams," he called out, walking out onto the back

porch as she was watering the plants. "I'm going to take a trip into town. I've got some explaining to do."

"I think that's a smart choice, Conner. I just hope they listen to what you have to say. You've got a lot to tell them, and they'd be fools not to listen," she said, hanging the hose over the plastic holder on the side of the house. "You just remember, if they don't listen to you, that's on them, not you."

Nodding, he turned to walk back inside. He needed to get a shower before heading anywhere.

"And, Conner," she called out after him, causing him to turn back to face her. "Make sure you come back here, please?"

"Yes, Grams, I will," he said, knowing how concerned she had been about him running from town. She wasn't the only one. Megan feared it too. He owed it to them both to stay put and take care of his trouble instead of running from it. That was exactly what he was going to do, starting with Adam.

But first, he needed a shower. No one needed to see him looking this rough. It was bad enough that Megan had to witness the look. The thought of Megan crossed his mind as he undressed and stood under the shower. The list of people he needed to talk to was but a few, but that list of three held two of the most important people to him.

THE DRIVE INTO TOWN WAS FULL OF EMOTIONAL thoughts and what-ifs. What if Adam didn't let him explain? What if Adam didn't believe Conner was trying to change?

He thought about pulling his phone out and giving his

brother a fair warning of his arrival but decided against it. He wanted to catch Adam off guard, hopefully in a good mood. If he gave him a heads-up, it meant Adam wouldn't be in a good mood and would instantly be pissed off.

Pulling into the parking lot at the station, he parked his truck and killed the engine. He wasn't planning on being here too long, but who knew how long it would take to get everything out and hopefully make amends.

Taking one last deep breath, he released it with a final push to get this over with—the sooner, the better. Climbing out of his truck, he didn't make it more than ten steps before he was face-to-face with Adam.

"What the hell are you doing here?"

There went the idea of not pissing Adam off prior to arriving. Record breaking time even. He'd have to write it down somewhere safe with his other personal bests—disappointing his father, ruining a friendship, responding to calls defiantly and disobeying the rules, and last but not least, losing his job and pissing his brother off. Oh, and having an issue with alcohol.

"I thought I'd come by and talk to you about everything. I've been away from the bottle..."

"For what? A day?"

Conner shrugged. The words stung, but he had them coming. He'd dealt with worse coming from his father. He could handle his brother's retaliation. "You're right, but it's a start. I can't make excuses for what I've done, been doing, but I can apologize and prove this isn't who I really am."

Desperation filled his words, making him sound pathetic, but it was the God's honest truth, so he had no problem saying what he had to say. There was no turning back now. He was there and he wasn't leaving until things were settled between them.

"Well, you've put on quite a show around here lately and I'm sure there's a laundry list of things going on that I have no idea about, right?" Adam's face twisted in anger as he folded his arms and held his stance inches from Conner's face.

"Actually, no, you're wrong. Everything that's been going on revolves around firefighting and this damn place," Conner said, jabbing a finger in the building's direction. He hated to think of how much damage he had done in his life, but the last thing he ever expected was his career to come to a complete halt. "I've tried to be the best, and unlike you, I make mistakes. I can't change who I am just for you. You can't see past the mistakes, then that's your problem, not mine. You think you can control everything in this life, you're wrong. You have no idea how good you've had it. Dad gave you everything. You barely had to lift a damn finger," Conner shouted, mad words spat out as he jabbed his finger into Adam's chest, who stood there without reaction. He'd expected his brother to knock him out—one punch and done—but it never happened. Instead, Adam listened with furrowed brows and arms down at his sides. "You have no idea what the hell I've gone through. You were put in charge here, but out there"—he pointed out west—"I was it. My crew and I. There was a chief and in command, but out there in the middle of those damn trees, it was me and them! That's it! It was my decision to go out there and it was my decision to chase those fires, but I'll be damned if you think for one minute I deserve everything that happened and is happening just because of the shit hand I was dealt! My friends, true friends, out there were like family. Better than family if you ask me."

"Are you done?" Adam asked calmly, hesitating to say anything more until Conner was said and done. He was far from it, but he was willing to give Adam a chance to say something, whatever that might be.

"For now, yeah," he said, stepping back and leaning against the hood of his truck. Looking around the parking lot for witnesses, he was thankful there weren't any. No one needed to see an altercation like this, especially between two brothers. It was pathetic, but it was something needing done.

"For one, if you don't recall, we have the same father, who raised us the same. I never had anything handed to me. I had to work for everything I own. Working my ass off and proving myself has gotten me to where I am now," Adam said. "You don't get to play victim when it comes to that. As far as making mistakes, I've made them too, but do you wanna know what the difference is between you and me?"

Conner couldn't care less what the difference was between them. Hell, he'd known it all along. Their age difference, along with their father favoring one over the other, the list could go on and on.

"I own up to my mistakes and learn from them, unlike you." Adam jabbed a finger in Conner's face and Conner had to restrain himself from coming unglued. "You come waltzing back in town like Mr. Bigshot and when push comes to shove, you fuck things up and want to run and hide. You, not me. So don't tell me I've got no idea what mistakes are, because I've made several. I just don't dwell on the damn things. I make them, I own up to them, and move the hell on."

Conner crossed his arms, waiting for Adam to continue with his frustrated rant. He kept his mouth shut, knowing if he opened it now, he wouldn't be listened to anyway. Might as well hear Adam out.

"And for the record, I don't think you deserve what

you've been handed. I know Colorado took a toll on you. I saw it in your face when you first came back. I'm your brother. As much as you hate that little fact, I care. Honestly, I care so much that it hurt me more than you to kick you out of here. You think I wanted to see my brother lose his job and have nowhere to go? If so, you're wrong. It was the last thing I wanted, but you didn't come around. You kept messing up, and that damn drinking got the best of you. You changed, but not for the better."

Damn, whoever said the truth hurt sure wasn't joking. Adam didn't waste any time sugarcoating shit. Conner was at a loss for words. He'd been so angry at Adam for doing what he had done, but now, he wasn't sure who to be more mad at—Adam or himself.

"You can't blame your actions on anyone but yourself. You can't come back to town thinking things are the same, because I don't know if you've realized it or not, but they're not. Things have changed a lot in the last two years. Hell, even our parents. Dad's memory isn't the greatest, and his health is fading fast, but still, things aren't the same. We're older and wiser now, or hell, we're supposed to be by now. I get it, you're struggling to cope with the bullshit, but maybe if you weren't so damn stubborn, you'd reach out for help and more than likely, you'd get it. Instead, you reached for the damn bottle and look where that got ya. Nowhere but without a job and another conflict to face."

He wasn't even pissed anymore. Adam had made several points and the only thing he heard in the whole rambling was his father's memory and health were fading fast. No one had told him about his father's health condition. Why the hell not? Just because they didn't talk didn't mean he didn't care. It was his father, for Christ's sake.

"When'd you find out about Dad?" he asked, pushing

off the hood of his truck. The thought of calling his dad crossed his mind, but he knew the guy wouldn't want to talk to him. There was nothing that had changed with that while everything else was changing. "How bad is he? What's going on?"

Adam shook his head, running a hand over his face. "Look, I shouldn't have said anything. It wasn't my business to tell."

"It's our dad," Conner pleaded, forgetting about everything else for the fact he cared more about his dad than all the other shit. "What's going on? Tell me, now, or I swear to God I'll—"

"He's got dementia. The doctor thinks it's more than likely Alzheimer's, but they won't know until it progresses."

"What? What the hell does that mean?" Conner had never been good with medical terms. He was a firefighter, he didn't need to know them. But now, his father had some sort of memory issue and it scared the shit out of him. "How long has he been dealing with it?"

Adam shrugged. "It's hard to say. Doctors think he's been living with it for a while now, but they can't say for sure."

"Damn. How bad is he?" He hated asking bluntly, but without direct communication with his dad in the last couple of years, he knew nothing and couldn't fathom something happening to his dad without making amends with him—with whatever part of his memory he had left.

"He's not *that* bad, but he's not good either. Mom says it's a constant flip of the switch. Between his memory loss and his mood swings, she doesn't know when he's coming or going. She's been dealing with it for a while now. The doctor says the mood swings are most likely associated with the frustration of the disease."

"You think he'll remember me?" Conner asked, feeling like his teenage self when he first disappointed his father. He'd been desperate for his father to forgive him and be proud of him. That was all he'd ever wanted.

"Conner, he's still got some of his memory. I'm sure he remembers you just fine."

"Good, maybe he'll remember why the hell we've been at each other's throats for so long," Conner said, grabbing his keys out of his pocket and heading to the driver's side of his truck before yanking the door open. "Because I sure as hell don't."

23

Megan had taken some time off from the station and Levy's. She had decided it was time to take a step back and focus on what was more important, and that was family. She wanted to hang out at the café. Helping Granny Mae and her grandmother was something she looked forward to when she woke up this morning. After her visit with Conner yesterday, she realized she needed to give him space and let him sort through things. He'd come around, and when he did, she would be right here waiting.

"Good morning, Meg," her grandmother called out as she walked into the diner just after eight o'clock. She had planned to be there sooner but sleeping in felt great. She had slept a full eight hours last night and it felt amazing. "Are you ready to drink some coffee and gossip with us oldies?"

Megan laughed, tossing her keys into her purse and hanging it over the corner of the booth she chose to sit in. "I suppose I could use some coffee and as far as gossip, I'm way out of the loop."

"That's good then, we've got plenty to talk about," Rosie patted her on the cheek and walked toward the coffee pot. Filling the mug with the steaming liquid of morning delight, she said, "Starting with Adam and Rachel's wedding. It's right around the corner and no one's got a clue where the wedding will be or even the reception. They're keeping everything top secret."

Megan smiled at the thought of planning a wedding and keeping it secret. She wondered how much simpler that would make things, or how complicated. It could definitely go both ways. Knowing her luck, it would be complicated and things would most likely fall apart before they were put together.

"So, Granny and I were thinking you could ask Rachel and see if you can get any information out of her," Rosie said, handing the coffee to Megan before walking to the booth Megan picked to sit in. "What do you say about that?"

"I say you and Granny are out of your minds," Megan said, laughing before taking a sip of the strong coffee. "You really think Rachel would tell me? Because I highly doubt I'd be anywhere on the list of people she'd tell. If she chose to tell anyone, it would be Leah, not me."

Rosie's eyes lit up. "Leah. Why didn't I think of that! I'll be right back!"

Megan watched her grandmother hurry off to the back room where if she had to guess, Granny Mae was either fixing up a nice breakfast, or eavesdropping on their conversation. Either way, Granny Mae was back there and it was confirmed when Granny Mae hollered out to Megan about her needing to talk to Leah for them.

"It'd be too obvious if us old coons were asking, because

you know Wes and Edward, and we're best friends with Ed's wife, Evelyn."

Megan rolled her eyes and shook her head. "Isn't there anything else you guys could be getting the scoop on instead of a wedding we'll be invited to soon enough?"

The bell above the door rang and in walked Conner.

"Hey," she called out to him, waving him over to her. "What's up?"

He slid into the open spot across from her and shrugged. "I just got told my father's got dementia, and he didn't answer my call." He shook his head. "Not that I was expecting him to. It's just hard to know he's got things going on and we're fighting. It's sad because I don't even know what the hell happened between us to cause such a lasting fight."

"Who told you about your dad?" she asked, but she figured it had to have been Adam, which meant one thing —Conner had gone to talk to Adam. She crossed her fingers this would bring good news, but right now, the focus was on his father and she needed to be his sounding board. One thing she noticed, aside from the concern etched deep on his face, he looked better than he did yesterday.

"I went to make things right between Adam and me. He was pissed, ranting about one thing then another, and it slipped out. I don't think he meant to tell me. I think it was to remain a secret between them."

"Did you find out about the wedding?" her grandmother asked, butting into their conversation without a single clue what they had been talking about. "I know it's a secret, but now I want to know what you know."

As if Granny's hearing aids were working far too well, she shuffled toward them and said, "If you're in on the secret, you better tell me. I wanted to be the first to know, but it looks like that's not going to happen."

Conner gave Megan a puzzled look. Megan shrugged and shook her head. "Grandma, he's not talking about the wedding."

"What?" Granny questioned. Near the booth and now her hearing faded, go figure. "You don't know the deets about the wedding either?"

Disappointment crossed Granny's face, but Megan couldn't help but laugh at her choice of words. A woman in her mid-sixties, or was it seventies, using words a teenager would most likely use when talking to their friends.

"Guys, can we have a minute or two alone?" Megan asked, trying hard to give Conner the space he needed.

"I knew it," Granny said, shaking a finger between them. "You two are the newest lovebirds in town. I called it! Rose, did you hear that? I knew it!"

Megan covered her face with her hands. How embarrassing. She peeked out at Conner, who was wearing the biggest shit-eating grin displaying his dimples. Of course he found this entertaining.

"Oh, Meg, there's nothing to be shy about," Granny said, patting Megan's hands while attempting to uncover her face. "We all knew the day would come when you two would realize how good you are for each other."

Megan shooed her away and laughed. Turning her attention back to Conner, she said, "I'm sorry about that. I have no idea what she's talking about. Anyway, back to what you were saying."

Conner laughed and shook his head. "It's nothing worth talking about right now. I'll talk to my dad sooner or later, but right now I want to talk about what Granny knows about us."

Cheeks turning beet red, Megan fanned her face with the menu card from the napkin holder. "I have no idea why she would say that. She has no idea."

Conner tipped his head back and laughed. It was good to see him laughing again. Just like old times when they would hang out together. The laughter had been endless back then.

"I think she does," Conner said, locking eyes with Megan. If the butterflies hadn't been swarming before, they definitely were now. "I'm pretty sure the whole town saw us coming before we did."

"What are you trying to say, Conner?" Her words caught in her throat and her heart beat so fast, she felt like it was about to slam out of her chest, making an escape before it had a chance to get hurt.

"I'm saying we should talk about us," he said, reaching across the table to take her hand in his. He smiled and once again those dimples of his caught her eye and she inhaled a deep breath. If he was ready to talk about them, then she wasn't going anywhere. Her feelings had never left. They were stronger than they'd ever been and with him holding her hand right now, she might have died and gone to heaven.

"I've got all day if you do," she said, laughing when he cocked his head to the side.

"Let's go for a ride," he said, pulling her hand as he slid out of the booth and waited for her to follow. Without hesitation, she was on her feet and chasing after him on the way to his truck. Wherever he would take them, she was along for the ride. With everything that had happened in the last few weeks, she was glad to see the old Conner next to her in the driver's seat as they headed out on the county road—destination unknown and she didn't care. She would go anywhere with Conner as long as he would have her there beside him, riding shotgun in his truck with a subtle glimpse of their future together as they traveled down the road.

"What do you have in mind?" she asked over the rev of the engine. Conner smiled, refusing to let her in on their last-minute escapade. "If it's where I think you're taking me, I'm going to love you forever."

He looked over at her, a grin bigger than Houston tugging at his lips. "Is that a promise?"

Nodding, she smiled as she leaned back and enjoyed the ride to their favorite place in the whole world. She would never forget this day for as long as she lived and her memory stayed with her. She couldn't wait for the outcome of this random getaway and by the look on his face, neither could he.

24

Keeping the suspense of where he was taking her alive and well, he drove the back way through the mountains. She never liked surprises, but this would be one he hoped she would love.

With everything happening recently, he wasn't able to act like himself. He had so much to tell her and with this last-minute decision to drive her out into the mountains, he could only hope things went in his favor.

Guiding the truck around the remaining curves, he smiled when the cabin came into view. It needed some fixing up, but it was a solid structure. He was more than ready to get started on it.

"What's this?" Megan asked, eyes wide as she pointed at the cabin sitting in front of them. "Whose is this?"

Conner couldn't help but smile at her excitement. He'd known for years he would own a cabin in due time, he just waited it out to find one he liked. This one had caught his eye when he was younger, but now, he was willing to stay in Cedar Valley and this was the perfect spot to live—in the middle of the woods with a morning view of the mountains.

"Mine," he said before she shrieked and hopped out of his truck. He climbed out and met her in the front. She was ecstatic, jumping up and down laughing.

"I can't believe it! It's really yours?"

He nodded and motioned for her to follow him up the front steps. The porch was small, but once he got a start on it, this place would have a wraparound porch, that way they'd get to sit wherever they'd like and enjoy the view on all sides of the cabin and not just one. He used the term *they* lightly as he thought about Megan moving in with him. He could only pray she'd say yes when the time was right. "Wanna see inside?"

He unlocked the door and swung it open. He held the door as she stepped past him, the surprise still having an effect on her facial expressions.

"This place is huge, Con," she said, arms held out wide as she spun in a complete circle inside the empty space in the living room. "This is really yours? How?" Her expression dropped and he knew the thought that had crossed her mind.

"Technically, my gramps helped me get it, with the promise that I'd stay put and work things out. He'd had his eyes on it for a while now, but he figured it'd be perfect for me. So, with his agreement to take payments, he got the loan and bought it," Conner explained, knowing his grandfather had been more than willing to get this place and have Conner pay him back little by little. "Honestly, I'm a little shocked myself."

He watched her inspect every room as they toured the place. He was happy to see her so excited. "But how are you going to make payments when you don't..." her words trailed off as she hesitated saying what she was thinking.

"Adam texted me right after I left the station, while I was sitting in Granny Mae's Café, actually," Conner said.

"So, what does that mean?" she asked, a look of concern crossing her face.

He didn't like that look on her. The last thing he wanted was for her to worry about him, even for a minute.

"It means I've got my job back," he said, catching her in his arms as she ran toward him. He twirled her around the open floor and in that instant, he realized what he'd had in front of him all along. "As long as I straighten up, I'm good to go."

He laughed and she followed suit, tipping her head back as he swung her around what would be the living room in no time at all. "That's great, Con. I'm so happy for you," she said. Her blue eyes caught his and he wanted nothing more than to kiss her in this moment. "I've missed you."

When she said *you*, he knew she meant the old him. They had been so close for so many years, and his traumatic experiences had created a gap between him and the ones he loved. It had gotten worse when he turned to alcohol instead of reaching out for actual help. The alcohol had drowned out the thoughts, but it'd been temporary. He needed a permanent way to get the thoughts to clear, and at the time he hadn't known a better way to cope. Now he knew and would be starting therapy once the weekend was over. This was his second chance, upon a million others, to get it right this time, and there wasn't anything he wanted more than to get it right. He was tired of failing. He wasn't a failure and he refused to fail now.

"I missed you too," he said, wrapping his arms around her, holding her for an extra minute. "I've missed you so much and I wish things would've been different. I'm sorry."

Looking up at him, she pulled back and said, "I know.

Me too. But all that matters is you're here now and you're not going anywhere."

Her words hit him deep. There was no way he could ever leave Cedar Valley again. He'd gone through hell the last time he'd left, and even though things had been rough for a while here, he'd come out of it stronger and knowing the difference between right and wrong. He was a work in progress, but he had promised Adam he wouldn't screw this up. He'd made the same promise to Gramps, too.

"Nope, I'm here for the long haul," he said, kissing the top of her head.

Taken by surprise, Megan pulled back and looked up at him. A questionable expression crossed her face and he felt actions would speak louder than words as he landed his lips on hers. She laughed and playfully pushed him away. "You didn't have to kiss me," she said, blushing with the biggest smile, revealing the cutest dimples he'd ever seen. "What was that for?"

She sure was cute when she was flustered. She couldn't get her words out and she was more than embarrassed she hadn't been ready. Trying to figure everything out at once, she stared at him, puzzled and wanting an explanation. All he wanted to do was kiss her again.

"Use your words, Conner," she said, snapping her fingers, the smile on her face not fading. "What the hell was that for? What does it mean?"

"I love you, Meg," he said, the words falling out in the open without control. He didn't regret saying them but wondered where the hell his control was when it came to having her here in front of him at this very minute. "I always have. Ever since that first day we met and I put a frog in your lunchbox, I've had these crazy feelings for you. My thoughts have never been right since."

Laughing, he thought of how she'd corrupted his thoughts when he hit adolescence and puberty skyrocketed. Man oh man, what he would never confess to her. But those were but a dream now coming true today and he couldn't be happier with her reaction to his words.

"You've liked me that long and you've kept it a secret from me?" she asked, jabbing a playful finger into his chest. "How could you?"

Holding up his hands, he said, "Whoa, now wait a minute, miss. How about you? How long have you known you liked me? You've kept it secret too, I suppose? For how long?"

Tapping a finger against her lips, she stopped to think about it. She was so serious about it, too. He could almost see the steam circling above her head as her thoughts raced. "I would like to say since I was about seven or eight, but I'm pretty sure it was way before then," she said, winking, followed by a laugh as she ran into his arms and pressed her lips to his.

"Then you're just as guilty, if not more, than I am," he said, tracing her jawline with the tip of his finger. She was so damn pretty.

"I plead the fifth," she said before grabbing his hand and pulling him through the rest of the house. "Show me the rest of this place. The view is beautiful."

Standing in front of the large bay window, he realized he could get used to this view as he wrapped her in his arms and pressed his lips against her temple. "You're much more beautiful than that view will ever be."

She laughed, pulling away from him. "*That* was cheesy," she said, still laughing as she made her way into the empty kitchen. "I still can't believe this place is yours. Honestly, I can't believe you love me and you have this huge cabin in the middle of the woods with a spectacular view of the mountains."

She danced around the kitchen, peeking out every window she passed by on her way to the dining area before heading up the stairs around the corner. "I don't know whether to be jealous of you or happy for you," she said, winking back at him as he climbed the stairs right behind her.

"Why don't you move in with me?" he asked, swallowing hard after the words spilled out. He didn't want to ask her so soon. Guess he still needed to work on that whole thinking before acting thing.

She reached the top landing and turned to face him. "Are you serious?"

He knew he'd asked too soon. He should have waited a while before rushing into anything. What the hell had he been thinking? "It's okay if you say no. I just figured we've been friends forever, and the love, well, I think..."

"Conner, I'd love to."

Now he was the one to be surprised and there was no way of hiding it. He could've sworn he'd blown it. There'd been so many doubts she would have said no way or get lost, but she hadn't. Things were getting better and better. Maybe his luck was changing after all.

25

She couldn't deny being surprised by Conner's cabin. The fact he had promised his grandfather to straighten up and stick around meant things were changing. He was willing to turn his life around and get his crap together.

And telling her he's loved her for however long had been music to her ears. Just to know he felt the same way she did was enough to make her happy—more than happy. Knowing now she wouldn't have to worry about messing up their friendship with telling him how much she loved him, she could tell him every day.

"Do you mind taking me into town?" she asked, regretting having to leave this bed and him, but she had things she needed to get done—one of those things involved talking with her grandma. She needed to make sure her grandma wasn't still mad about her staying on the fire department. She loved what she did, but her grandma was the last person who would ever like it or approve of it. The last thing she wanted was to be disrespectful in her grandmother's thoughts and feelings, so she needed to make sure everything was okay between them.

"Are you sure you want to leave this nice, warm bed?" Conner tossed the sleeping bag over her head and tugged her down next to him. Their makeshift bed included two sleeping bags and pillows he'd had on standby just in case they ended up staying the night. It was a smart move on his part, more like premeditation, because the last thing she wanted to do last night was leave. The cabin was gorgeous although it was still missing things, but they made do with what they could find. It was nice to play house and think about what their future would hold—together as a couple and not just best friends. "But if you're absolutely sure you wanna leave, I'll run you to town after I get a shower. I'm thinking it's time for me to make a stop by my parents' house and make amends with my dad."

She wondered how that would play out. His father had held onto a grudge for so long now, it was almost impossible to think he'd let it go. Maybe the time would finally come and things could be settled. She could only hope, especially knowing his father's memory was fading. "I think that's a good idea."

Conner shrugged, doubt pulling at his expression. "It's worth a try, I guess. I'm not sure if he'll even talk, or listen to me, but I guess I'll find out soon enough, right?"

Megan nodded. "Trying anything is better than not at all. At least you'll know you tried one last time to make things right, and if it doesn't go the way you want it to, it won't be your fault."

She wasn't good at advice. She had struggled many times over her own personal dilemmas between her family, but in the end, if it's meant to work out, it'll work out. Having faith and hoping for the best was the only thing a person like them could do. She hoped for Conner's sake that the time was right and his father would open up to him. They needed to make amends and forgive each other while forgetting the past, along with the differences between them.

The thought of being by Conner's side while he went to talk to his father crossed her mind, but she knew they'd be better off alone in discussion without anyone witnessing the hard truths that had separated them for the last several years.

Conner dropped her off at the diner and headed west toward his parents' house. She wished him luck and told him to call her if he needed to. Otherwise they'd see each other tonight at Adam and Rachel's house.

The wedding was right around the corner and they still had no idea what Adam and Rachel had planned for it. They hadn't received invites, even though they knew they would be invited regardless of receiving a piece of paper or not. She was excited to see the two get married. A long time coming for them and she couldn't wait to celebrate with them.

Pushing through the diner's door, the bell rang above her head, announcing her arrival before she was greeted by an overly excited grandmother and Granny Mae as they stood by the counter, playing cards. The tables were empty, leaving the diner completely vacant.

"Megan, I thought you were with Conner," Granny Mae called out, smiling a shit-eating grin, knowing full well she was on the money. It was almost like she was calling out *she knew it* as she nudged Rosie's arm. "What brings you in here?"

Megan walked to the counter, shoving her phone into her back pocket before climbing onto her favorite stool next to the cash register. "I figured I would swing in here for a bit while Conner heads over to talk to his dad."

Granny's eyes widened and Megan realized she'd said too much. After closing her gaping mouth, Granny shuffled toward the empty seat next to Megan. Megan reached a hand over to help Granny as she slid onto it, but the woman swatted her hand away. "I'm old but not *that* old."

Cracking up laughing, the two of them hugged each other. Rosie had made a reappearance from the kitchen with a fresh pot of coffee and a plate of food. She shrugged as she set them on the counter in front of Megan. "I figured you're hungry and needing some coffee."

"Thanks, Grandma," Megan said, accepting the offering as she poured herself a cup. She'd lost quite a bit of sleep last night and she blamed Conner for that. She smiled at the memory.

"I see that smile," Granny said, pinching her cheek. "Is that smile because of Conner? Please say yes."

Megan laughed, nearly spitting her coffee out. Granny's persistence to play matchmaker was something they'd miss when the woman was gone. The memories they'd shared were something she'd never forget when the day came to say goodbye, but for right now, she didn't want to think about it. Granny Mae had become a part of the family.

"I take that as a yes?"

"Yes," Megan admitted, waiting for Granny to fall off her chair laughing, admitting she'd been right this whole time. "He showed me his cabin last night. It's beautiful out there."

"Is that the only thing he showed you?" Granny asked, laughing while trying so hard to be serious.

Rosie reached across the counter, swatting a towel in Granny's direction. "Cut it out," she said, failing at not laughing herself. "There won't be none of that. Right, Megan?"

Megan took a bite of her eggs, stuffing her mouth full as she nodded her response. What Rosie didn't hear, didn't hurt her.

"Edward helped him with that cabin," Granny said, stirring creamer into her cup of coffee. "I think that was a wise decision on his part. And I also think that boy'll prove he's worth the trouble he's been having lately. Everyone makes mistakes, some bigger than others. That doesn't make them a bad person. A bit immature, yes, but not bad at all."

Megan nodded, taking another bite of food. She hadn't realized she was so hungry until the smell of food lingering in front of her wafted through her senses. She was thankful she had this diner to come to for breakfast. They served the best in town—okay, maybe they were the only place in town, but still.

"I think he's a good kid, too," Rosie chimed in, keeping her eyes on Megan while finishing up her coffee. "I just want to make sure he doesn't risk my granddaughter's life to save his pride."

Megan couldn't argue with her. She had a point. There were a few times Megan had questioned Conner's intentions and common sense. She knew he had gone through so much in Colorado, but that didn't excuse his reckless behavior here in Cedar Valley. There were consequences to face for every action a person took, and for firefighters, that meant losing trust, or worse, life and death.

"There were times when I wanted nothing more than to

drag you out of that service, but I knew I couldn't," her grandmother said, making another pot of coffee. They definitely went through the first pot quite fast, but it tasted good and helped wake them up. "I mean, who am I but a grandma? You're smart and good at what you do, but it just scares me to think you'd risk everything to save that man."

Megan knew, once again, her grandmother had a well-established point. Megan would do anything to save anyone, regardless of the risks to her own life. It was a chance she took every day when it came to her job, but she wasn't going to tell her grandmother that.

"Megan, you've got to understand there are some things worth that risk," Rosie said, frowning as she stirred her coffee. "You got lucky that day you ran in after him. I know you know that, and like I said, I know I'm no one except some old lady with an opinion, but I love you and want you to be okay. I don't want to have to worry about you keeping safe on these calls. You proved you know your stuff and you can do the job, but I want you to promise me you'll keep your emotions out of the way when push comes to shove."

Megan finished the food on her plate and attempted to carry it to the back, but Rosie grabbed it, offering to do it for her. Megan sat back down.

Granny patted her leg and smiled. "You know she's right," Granny Mae said. "She wants her baby safe, is all."

Megan nodded and watched her grandmother walk back to her seat. "Grandma, I promise to always be careful on calls. I wouldn't have done anything you or Wes wouldn't have done for each other. I never let my emotions interfere with my job, but I also make sure and do my job. Sure, I was wrong for putting my neck on the chopping block when it came to Conner and Adam, but Conner's a good guy. He'd tried so hard to do the right thing and prove he was able to fit in around here," Megan said, shrugging while thinking about how foolish it had been to stand up to her boss the way she had. At most, it was unprofessional and proved she allowed emotion to overrule her thought process. "I didn't want to see him go down like he did."

"I understand, but I don't want to see you go down either," Rosie said, patting Megan's hand. "As long as you promise me you'll be careful on every call, there's nothing I can do. I stand beside you in everything you do, and have done. I won't stop now."

"Thank you," Megan said, running a finger around the rim of her cup. "Have either of you heard about where the wedding is going to be or is it still a *top secret* event we aren't supposed to know about?"

"We haven't heard a thing and haven't a clue," Rosie said, looking at Granny Mae for affirmation, who in turn shrugged her shoulders and shook her head. "Not a word has been said to either of us."

Megan wondered what the heck was up Rachel's sleeve, err wedding dress.

"Last I heard, Leah has been spending a lot of time at the community center this last week or so," Granny Mae said, offering her shit-eating grin once again. "I'm thinking she's the one decorating for the wedding and I've got a feeling it might be happening sooner than we think."

Megan knew Leah would make a great bridesmaid. As the best friend of the bride, she'd make sure everything would go as planned. Leah had such a way with decorating and planning, Megan bet she'd make a good wedding planner, too. Maybe one day, Megan would hire Leah to do just that for her wedding.

26

Hesitation and doubt filled Conner as he drove west out of town. He knew what he needed to do, but the doubt lingered in his mind. His father had been so stubborn, and like Conner, he refused to listen when others tried to prove him wrong.

Conner couldn't remember a time when they'd had a decent conversation without pointing fingers in blame or argument. It seemed ridiculous to know it'd been too long since they'd enjoyed each other's time together. Instead, the memories they'd shared were those of hurt and disappointment, which would later turn to regret and despair once his father's health faded to nothing and the good Lord called him home.

Conner swiped a fallen tear off his cheek, wondering since when a grown man would cry, but the thought of losing his father seemed to haunt him more these days than it ever had before.

Pulling into the driveway, he tried to not imagine his father's face once he answered the door. Maybe he would get lucky and his mother would answer, invite him in, and tell him they'd been wondering when he would stop by. Laughing, because the thought seemed too farfetched and not realistic, he shifted the truck into park and killed the engine.

Taking a minute to gain enough courage to make his way to the door, he stared out the windshield, wondering how long it had been since he'd been here last. Remembering it had been around Thanksgiving when he'd told them he was coming back home for good, a bittersweet memory played like a broken record in his mind.

Finally talking himself into it, he opened the door and stepped out. Gravel crunched under his boots as he closed the door behind him, second-guessing his decision the moment he let go of his truck handle.

Inhaling a deep breath, he slowly released it as he made his way to the door. One solid step at a time, he walked onto the porch. He still had time to turn around and leave. He could back out and they wouldn't know he had ever been there. Except they did know, because right when he chickened out and was about to turn around, the door swung open and he was met by his mother, who screamed and ran out into his arms. It was the most awkward but relieving moment he had least expected.

"I'm so glad you're here. I've been so worried about you," she whispered, her words muffled by his shirt. "I've been wanting to call you, just to talk to you, but I didn't know what to—"

"Mom, it's okay," he said, hugging her tighter against him, reassuring her she didn't do anything wrong. It was him. He should've never lost contact with her in the first place, but stubborn is what stubborn does and it wasn't her fault. "I'm here now and I'm sorry. I should've never left you like that. I'm sorry."

Sniffling, followed by wiping away tears, his mom let go of him and said, "It's okay. We're okay."

She patted him on the arm and led him into the house. Hesitation returned for a split second, but he knew it could end one of two ways, and the second way was nothing that hadn't happened before. He'd mentally prepared himself for the worse-case scenario.

Ready or not, it was now or never.

Walking into the living room, he hadn't been prepared quite enough for the sight of his father. Who would have known a failing memory could make one look so rough? Not him, that's for sure. He hated to think of how long they'd have left together before his memory completely failed him, making him forget who his sons were, or even his wife of nearly fifty years.

"How bad is he?" Conner whispered, turning back to his mother, having one last thought to act on his escape before it was too late.

"I'm not that bad." His father's voice boomed behind him, causing Conner to turn slowly, knowing full well his father was completely coherent of what was happening around him. "Yet."

His father sounded ten years older than the last time he had heard him speak. The frail looking man sat in his recliner, with a tobacco pipe sticking out of his mouth. Hell, with a brain failing, what could tobacco hurt?

"Hey, Dad," he said, reentering the living room, taking his time as if there were eggshells waiting to be broken under his feet.

"Hey yourself," his father replied, gesturing for Conner to hurry up and sit down.

Conner took the invitation before his father changed his mind.

"What's been going on with you lately?"

Conner tried to hide his surprise, wondering if this was a side effect of the memory loss. Maybe he didn't remember the ongoing tension-filled conflict between them. Conner sat down at the end of the couch, making sure to sit forward while facing his father.

"I've heard quite a bit about you lately," his father said, chuckling as he leaned back in his chair. "You've been quite the star around here."

Conner didn't like the sound of that. He'd thought his father was inviting him in to have an actual conversation with him. This wasn't starting out too promising. "I wouldn't say that. I just did what I thought was right, but honestly, I'm not sure I really know what that is anymore."

His father nodded, pulling a drag from his pipe before saying, "You'll learn in time. You've come a long way since I was chief, but you've got a long way to go."

Hating to hear those words, especially from his father, Conner crossed his arms. He wasn't quite sure how much further he'd have to go to prove he knew his shit, but according to his father, he wasn't quite there yet, go figure.

Regretting coming, Conner wanted to stand up and walk out, but then his father caught him by surprise. "I was once just like you, ya know?"

No, he didn't know. He had no idea how his father had once been because the two had never seen eye to eye long enough to discuss their similarities, only their differences.

"I was once young and impatient to prove my worth on the service," his father explained, taking another drag from his pipe. "But, like you, it bit me in the ass. I know it's hard to believe, but it's the God's honest truth. And I guess what I'm trying to say is you just never know how much you've got to learn until your ignorance of the situation smacks you in the face. It's a part of growing up, but also a part of learning the dos and don'ts in this life we live. We set our eyes on the prize, the unrecognized efforts of doing our jobs, that sometimes we fail to see what really matters. Trust me, I've been there, done that. And I think that's why I've been the way I am toward you because I see so much of me in you and it scared me. I refused to accept I've done the same exact things you've been doing, and I judged you a bit too harsh for it and I'm sorry."

Shocked by his father's confession, Conner sat silently, waiting for the *but* to follow, but it never came. Instead, his father put out his pipe, setting it aside, as tears welled in his eyes. "I'm glad you stopped by today, son. I've been wanting to call you, invite you to go fishing sometime to clear this bullshit between us, but since you're here, why wait, right?" A chuckle escaped as he blew out the remaining smoke from his last drag. Tears welled, glistening in his father's eyes, and Conner couldn't help but wonder when his father had come to his senses about this unresolved conflict between them. He guessed it really didn't matter now, because it was being taken care of and that was all that mattered. "Say, you wouldn't happen to have some spare time on your schedule, would ya? What do you say about going fishin' with your old man?"

Conner shrugged. "I could probably clear it and make some changes."

"That would be good, son," his father said, sitting forward after shoving the reclining part of the chair down. "I'm sure you've heard my memory ain't as good as it used to be."

Conner nodded. Regretfully so, he'd heard the news and that was what prompted this visit, but he wasn't going to tell his father that. Some things needed to remain unsaid. It was better that way.

"You never know, I might forget how to fish," he said. Another laugh followed his words. "That wouldn't be too good, would it?"

Again, Conner shook his head and wondered why this conversation was going so well. He couldn't help but wait for the other shoe to drop. Something bad always came with something good. He always believed in the saying *if something's too good to be true, then it probably is.* Suspicion weighed heavy on his mind as he watched his father's excitement about fishing and catching up with Conner.

"You know you had your mother worried when you made that brave rescue of the little boy in that house fire, right?" his father asked, pointing in his mother's direction. "But I told her you'd be all right. And you were, weren't ya? I'd been right, because I knew what I would have done in that situation, and I knew you're so much like me that you would've acted on that split second decision of yours. That's the day I realized how proud I am of you, son. So damn proud."

Conner had no words. To hear his father describe his thoughts on what could've been a fateful day, it shocked him to say the least. He wanted nothing more than to make his father proud of him. To make his father not question his decisions or actions, but instead be proud for what he chose to do regardless of the consequences.

"I've been hardheaded and stubborn in the last few years," his father explained, "but I want you to know that's on me, not you. You didn't do anything wrong. Nothing was your fault. This feud between us, or whatever the hell it was, it was wrong. I should've never let it go on this long. Your mother let me have an earful every night your name had been brought up. I knew in my heart I'd make it right someday, and I'm glad that someday became today. Not that I'm trying to justify my actions or say what I did was right. Not at all. I just hope you can forgive me and we can move forward."

His father stood from his chair, walked over to where Conner was sitting, extended his hand, and once Conner grabbed onto it, he pulled Conner from the couch and embraced him in the strongest hug Conner had felt in a long time.

"I love you, son," his father said, "don't ever forget that."

"I love you, too, Dad."

EPILOGUE

Waking up to the view of the mountains would never get old, and neither would loving Conner. They had come so far, as friends and as lovers, and she had so much to be thankful for. She hated to think of how things would have been had he not made his way back home, or if he hadn't decided to stay here in Cedar Valley for good.

"Are you ready?" Conner hollered to her from their living room. She had spent the last few minutes looking in the mirror, deciding if she liked herself in a dress. The only time she'd ever worn a dress had been to church when she was younger. Since then, she'd been a tomboy, wearing short shorts and cowgirl boots, but getting dirty had been her specialty. "I promise you look fine. More than fine," he said, now standing right outside the bathroom door. "You look beautiful and I can't wait to get you home later to ravish you. I'll rip it off you."

Laughing, she opened the door and jumped into his arms. "If you're trying to earn points, you're racking them up." She kissed his lips as he swung her around in his arms. "But you're still cheesier than all get out."

"But you love me," he said, winking before setting her down with a peck on the cheek. "What do you say we get to this wedding before they start wondering where the best man and bridesmaid snuck off to?"

"Sounds like a plan," she said, hooking her arm through his as they made their way down the stairs.

She couldn't wait until it was her wedding they were going to. Of course, they wouldn't be able to see each other beforehand, with bad luck and all, or so they said, but she wasn't risking anything to find out.

The church was full of friends and family, from the front to the back, standing room only as Megan and Conner made their way to the front. Offering friendly waves, they smiled their way to the altar. Rachel and Adam looked out into the crowd, watching Megan and Conner as they approached. Megan smiled and waved, excited to hug Rachel and congratulate her when things were all said and done.

Splitting up at the altar, Conner made his way to his brother's side while Megan stood next to Rachel. She couldn't help but notice the crumpled piece of paper in Rachel's hands. The words *My Vows* lined the top, followed by several lengthy lines filled the page.

Megan smiled, knowing that was exactly what she wanted to do at her wedding. Custom vows were so special and she would want Conner to know exactly what that moment meant to her when she was standing at the altar, waiting to marry the man of her dreams.

The preacher man wed the couple, allowing them to say their vows, and announced them husband and wife. There wasn't a dry eye in the room as the husband kissed his wife.

Watching the newlywed couple walk down the aisle and exit the church, Megan turned to Leah, who was sobbing uncontrollably. Megan blamed it on the pregnancy hormones, as she stood next to Leah with her arms tugging her close. "Aww, don't cry. She still loves you."

Leah laughed, sniffled, and laughed some more. "I know that. It's just, I never thought this day would come for her and it finally did. They're so good for each other."

THE RECEPTION FOLLOWED THE WEDDING. CARS LINED the highway as they made their way to the community center. Megan couldn't wait to see the decorations Leah had done to prepare for this special day.

Conner reached across the bench seat of his truck and brought her closer to him. She felt the warmth against her as he wrapped an arm around her shoulders. "I love you, Megan."

"I love you, too." She smiled at how easy the words came for them. This whole relationship seemed so easy for them. Something she was more thankful for every passing day.

"Can I promise you something?" he asked, kissing the top of her head as he guided the truck down the highway.

She nodded against him.

"I promise one day soon this will be us."

She sat up and looked into his eyes. Tears filled hers and he wiped them away with a swipe of his thumb. Lips trembling, tears flowing, she sat speechless before he pulled the truck over onto the side of the road.

"What are you doing? We've got to get to the reception. They'll be waiting for us."

Shifting into park, he pressed play on the radio and climbed out, pulling her out with him. A smile on his face, he took her hands and dropped to one knee. "Megan, I love you with all my heart and I promise to love you for as long as I live. There's no doubt in my mind how far our love will take us, and for that I'm thankful. I'll be forever thankful for your friendship, your love, and your saving grace," he said, smiling up at her, squeezing her hands tight. "Megan, will you marry me?"

"Yes, Conner," she said. "Yes, I'll marry you!"

Sliding the ring onto her finger, he stood and wrapped her in his arms. Pulling her close, they danced to their favorite song while cars continued to drive by, honking as they passed.

"I love you, Megan."

"I love you more."

If you enjoyed Conner & Megan's story, please consider leaving a review on Amazon and Goodreads.

Thank you!

Christina

ALSO BY CHRISTINA BUTRUM

FAIRSHORE SERIES

Second Chances

Unexpected Chances

Fair Chances

CEDAR VALLEY SERIES

All She Ever Wanted

Everything She Needed

All She Ever Desired

KATE'S DUET

Kate's Valentine

Kate's Forever

STANDALONE NOVELS

No Place Like Home: Love in Seattle

Saving Jenna

Christina Butrum launched her writing career in 2015 with the release of The Fairshore Series.

Writing contemporary fiction, she brings realistic situations with swoon-worthy romance to the pages - allowing her readers to fall in love right along with the characters.

When she isn't busy writing, Christina enjoys spending time with her family. Christina Butrum looks forward to publishing many more books for her readers to enjoy.

Connect Below!

facebook.com/authorcbutrum

twitter.com/authorcbutrum

instagram.com/authorcbutrum

pinterest.com/christinabutrum

Made in the USA
Columbia, SC
17 September 2018